Dominating the expansive Dallas skyline, the Ewing Oil building testifies to the towering strength of the Ewing family. Beginning with Jock Ewing's struggle to build the company, and his sons' efforts to see it prosper and survive in uncertain times, DALLAS tells the story of the Ewing empire—its heartaches, joys, fears, and rage...

Series Story Editor *Mary Ann Cooper* is America's foremost soap opera expert. She writes the nationally syndicated column *Speaking of Soaps*, is a contributor to leading soap opera magazines, and has appeared as a guest on numerous radio and television talk shows.

Writers *Paul Mantel* and *Avery Hart* are, between them, the authors of plays, children's records, educational cassettes, and humor articles. They live in New York City, but have come to think of Dallas as their second home.

Dear Friend,

Welcome to the wonderful world of Soaps & Serials Books. Pioneer Communications Network, Inc., has gathered a great team of romance writers to recapture the excitement of all the best stories of daytime and nighttime drama in paperback novels. Now, from its very beginnings, relive the trials and tribulations of the Ewing clan as they play power politics in DALLAS.

Book 1, *Love Conquers Fear*, introduces us to the budding marriage of Bobby and Pam Ewing. Against all odds, these lovers believed that they could shut out the rest of the world and hold fast to their happiness. But naturally, J.R. soon shows them that honeymoons don't last forever. You'll enjoy every second of it. And after this, don't miss Book 2 of the DALLAS series, *Ardent Memories*.

For Soaps & Serials Books,

Mary Ann Cooper

Mary Ann Cooper

P.S. Write to me at Pioneer Communications Network, Inc., 825 Brook Street, Rocky Hill, CT 06067. I'd love to tell you about all our Soaps & Serials paperback novels.

DALLAS™

LOVE CONQUERS FEAR

From the television series created by David Jacobs

Soaps™ & Serials

PIONEER COMMUNICATIONS NETWORK, INC.

Acknowledgments

The publisher wishes to express his appreciation to Joseph S. Whitaker and Daniel J. Simon, of Lorimar Productions Licensing Division, for their belief in our concept and their continuing assistance and support in developing this series of books. Special thanks also to Christina Hampson.

Love Conquers Fear

From the television series DALLAS™ created by David Jacobs. This book is based on scripts written by David Jacobs.

DALLAS™ paperback novels are published and distributed by Pioneer Communications Network, Inc.

SOAPS & SERIALS™ is a trademark of Pioneer Communications Network, Inc.

ISBN: 0-916217-81-7

Printed in the United States of America

10 9 8 7 6 5 4 3 2 1

LOVE
CONQUERS
FEAR

Chapter One

The day was hot and steamy. Raoul, watching from the servants' entrance, could see the vapors rising from the patio by the pool. He wiped his brow with his already-wet handkerchief as he waited for Teresa to bring him the tray with the drinks. Glancing down at his starched uniform, he pondered the fact that if the heat wave lasted much longer, he was going to need a few extra shirts. Ah, well, at least things were quiet around Southfork. One had to be grateful for that.

Teresa came in from the kitchen with the drinks, tall and cool, accompanied by slices of lemon and orange, sprigs of mint and red swizzle sticks. Raoul thought how nice it would be to be rich like the Ewings, and to be able to sit by the pool on a summer Sunday drinking a cool drink and not having to work all day. But then, he wouldn't have been a Ewing for anything, he told himself. Too many troubles, too many fights. No, life was not easy for his employers. not easy at all, in spite of their enormous wealth.

Teresa gave him the tray and straightened his bow tie. Her beautiful brown eyes seemed to dance in her face, and she smiled a smile of promise. Tonight...ah, tonight they would go dancing at Crazy Pedro's, and then... then...he looked at her with longing. The heat always did that to a person, he thought. It tired the mind but inflamed the passions. Teresa gave him a quick but passionate kiss, then turned him around and headed him out the door. Tonight was one thing, today was another.

As Raoul walked down the path that followed the back of the mansion, the sounds of the Ewings grew louder with the blare of Miss Lucy's radio, as it played that horrible rock and roll music she loved so much, and the splashing of Mister Bobby and his pretty new wife, Pamela, as they swam their long, slow laps in the pool. They seemed so happy with each other, those two. Their love was like a breath of fresh air in the otherwise stifling atmosphere of Southfork Ranch. Raoul felt warm toward them, and worried for them, too. Happiness was a fragile commodity at Southfork.

He reached Mr. Jock first. The head of the clan was engaged in a game of backgammon with his wife, Miss Ellie. From the look on his face, Raoul could tell that Jock was losing again. If only he didn't take games so seriously. But then, Jock Ewing took everything in life seriously. That was probably why he had been so successful in life, building a multi-million dollar empire from nothing. His seriousness had brought him so much, but how much it had cost him!

Jock took a glass from the tray, without even

looking up, and immediately took a swig from it. Miss Ellie watched him disapprovingly, her sad blue eyes gazing out from under her sun hat at her husband. She worried about his health. He drove himself so—and he wasn't a young man anymore. Handsome and virile, yes, but not young.

"Don't think that's going to change your luck, Jock," she said, trying to be as tactful as possible.

Jock Ewing's frown deepened. Reaching for the dice, he replied, "I'll make my own decisions, thank you." And, throwing the dice violently, he moved his pieces around the board.

"I don't think you want to make that move," said his wife, unable to stop herself from responding to his challenge.

"This is backgammon, not college. Roll the dice."

"It *was* backgammon." Miss Ellie moved her piece off the board, ending the game. She took a drink from the tray with a flourish and turned away.

"You are the luckiest woman," murmured Jock, and signaled Raoul for another drink, which Jock put by the side of his chair where his wife wouldn't see it.

Now Raoul moved on to the others. He counted the drinks. There were still enough for everyone. Good for Teresa, he thought. She knew her employers well, down to the last detail.

Sue Ellen Ewing looked up from her crossword puzzle and took a drink from Raoul. How beautiful she was, thought Raoul, as beautiful as when she was crowned Miss Texas. That must have been seven, eight years ago, he remembered. She had aged well, no doubt about that. It was hard for a man to stop looking at her, especially in her revealing bathing suit. But Raoul didn't allow himself to look at her for too long. A servant had to know his place or find another job.

"Five letters...'floating signals'." Sue Ellen looked over at her husband, dozing on his chaise, and took a dainty sip from her glass.

J.R. Ewing opened his eyes, just a little. His body, broad and masculine, if just a touch overweight, was sprawled lazily on the chaise. But his eyes were as alert as lasers, and the wheels behind them turned relentlessly, even in his sleep. His sister-in-law, Pam, was treading water, chest-high, right in his line of vision. Her full, proud breasts bobbed up and down in the pool as she playfully splashed water at her husband. "Buoys," said J.R., and, taking a drink from the tray, he closed his eyes again.

"Right you are," said Sue Ellen, not a little annoyed. She had not been unaware of her husband's glance at Pamela. Suddenly the rock music blaring from the radio was unbearable to her. Raising her voice just a touch more than necessary, she turned to her niece and said, "Lucy, darling, would you mind lowering the volume just a touch, please?"

Lucy tossed her long blonde hair and took her lemonade from Raoul. Without a word in reply, she reached down and turned her radio up, just enough to answer for her. "Thanks, Raoul," she said with a wry grin. Taking out an applicator, she began to paint her toenails a very bright shade of red.

Raoul could not help grinning, too, much as he hated the music. It gave him pleasure to see Sue

Ellen needled. Everything about her was so perfect, every hair in place, her makeup perfectly applied. It was good to see her get her come-uppance every now and then. Partially to hide his amusement, Raoul bent down and deposited the two remaining drinks at the poolside table where Bobby and Pam could get them when they finished their swim. Then he began collecting the empty glasses and used napkins for his trip back to the kitchen.

Sue Ellen had not stopped staring at Lucy. "Lucy, I thought I asked you to *please* turn that music down."

"Didn't you say turn it up?" came the reply.

"No."

Lucy held the nail polish applicator up in the air and stared at it as if it were keeping her from complying with Sue Ellen's wishes. "I will, in a while," she said indifferently.

Sue Ellen turned back to her crossword in quiet fury. "That girl is spoiled to the core," she murmured to herself.

In the pool, Bobby and Pam had begun a mock swimming race. Bobby had been a champion swimmer at SMU, but Pam was matching him stroke for stroke, her lithe, supple body cutting the water like a knife. Jock Ewing looked up from his chair, and his brow wrinkled in concern. It hadn't been very long since her miscarriage, and Jock didn't want her to do anything to jeopardize her future as a childbearer. The Ewings needed heirs, and Sue Ellen hadn't succeeded in getting pregnant in seven years. It had taken Pamela only a couple of months, and if it hadn't been for that fight between Bobby and J.R., she might still be pregnant today. Jock could contain himself no longer. "Take it easy, now...Pam..."

Miss Ellie took his hand and patted it. "Don't worry so much, Jock," she said reassuringly.

"She shouldn't be working up a sweat," Jock protested, "she's still not healed..."

"She knows how much she can take, I'm sure," Miss Ellie said with finality, putting an end to the discussion. If Jock would worry about his own health the way he worried about his daughter-in-law's, she reflected, she wouldn't have to worry about him so much.

Jock looked at the two young people in the pool for another moment, and then, as if to distract himself from deeper concerns, he began setting up the backgammon board.

"Not another game, Jock," said Ellie. "You haven't won in six months!" She had to laugh. He was such a lovable pig-headed man.

"Five months," he corrected her, and threw the dice.

Pam and Bobby, having finished their race, emerged from the pool panting and laughing. Holding hands, they sauntered over to the table where Raoul had left their drinks. The droplets rolled down their strong young bodies as they walked, and the strength of their love for each other radiated out from them, washing over everyone at poolside. As they passed Jock's chair, he looked up and said, "Pam, don't you think you're overdoing it?"

Pam didn't break stride or even look at her father-in-law. "I'm all right," she said, barely taking the trouble to disguise her dislike. Jock Ewing had destroyed her father, and it was bad enough she had to live under the same roof with him. She certainly wasn't going to be nice to him, too.

As Pam dried herself, she found herself humming along with the song that had just come on the radio. Thank God for Lucy, she thought. She's the only one here who fights back. "That really is a good song," she said, smiling. Lucy looked over at Pam and, gazing into her eyes with a look of pure spite, turned the radio down. Pam sighed and shook her head. She knew how Lucy felt. She often felt the same way herself. The Ewings had destroyed Lucy's father the same way they'd destroyed her own. The girl's overwhelming anger was only natural. The wonder was that things had been so calm for so long. Turning to her husband, Pam asked quietly, "Is all this politeness going to go on forever?"

Bobby Ewing bent over and kissed his wife softly on the lips. "Enjoy it, Pammy. You know it's not liable to last."

Pam scowled, looking over at Jock, and then at J.R. "It's lasted much too long for my taste," she said.

Sue Ellen, as if she had heard her sister-in-law's words and was eager to oblige, put down her crossword puzzle and looked over at her niece. "Lucy, sweetheart, I understand you're going to the cattle auction tomorrow. You must be so excited." Lucy did not reply. She knew her aunt was trying to bait her, but she'd be damned if she'd lower herself to so petty a level as Sue Ellen's.

Miss Ellie, however, seemed oblivious to Sue Ellen's sarcasm. She longed for family harmony with such a passion that she seized on anything pleasant she could find. "I used to be crazy about those auctions," she said brightly. "My father used to take me with him."

Bobby looked up in surprise. "I can't believe it! Grandpa Southworth? He always used to say how this or that was or wasn't expected of a real man ... or a real lady. I figured cattle auctions wouldn't be on the list for ladies in Grandpa Southworth's book of rules." He trailed off with a chuckle. Ranching had certainly changed since his grandfather's day. But the thought of his mother as a pioneer of the women's movement made him laugh out loud. He looked over at her. Even at her age, she was the picture of old-fashioned Texas womanhood. Despite her petite frame, there was something regal about her, and the thought of her dirtying her hands at a cattle auction was as incongruous as could be.

Miss Ellie smiled at the wonder on her son's face. "Problem was, Daddy had a lot of trouble saying no to me."

Lucy couldn't resist. "Grandpa has the same trouble with Bobby." Everyone fell silent. The truth of her statement cut like a knife through everyone. But Miss Ellie was caught up in her reverie, and she continued as if Lucy hadn't spoken.

"When I was five or six years old and discovered what the auctions were about, I got very upset about it. I was mortified that they would sell any of our livestock."

Pam felt herself charmed by Miss Ellie in spite of herself. No matter what Jock Ewing had taken from her daddy—and he had taken plenty, including Miss Ellie—she couldn't hold Ellie to blame for what had happened. And, to be fair, Miss Ellie had welcomed her to Southfork with her whole heart. "If that's the case, why'd he take you with him? Wouldn't it have been better if you didn't see them being sold?"

"It didn't work out that way..." mused Miss Ellie, staring off into the past, "because there was another element to it—my Southworth pride. Once the auction had gotten underway, and people were bidding, I got very excited. It was important that our steer bring the highest price. After all, we always were famous for having the best livestock in Texas."

"And it's still true today, except it's Ewing livestock," Sue Ellen chimed in.

"It's difficult," admitted Miss Ellie, coming down from her cloud, "but we're doing our best."

Jock nodded. He had recently retired from Ewing Oil, turning it over to his eldest son, J.R., and devoted himself to ranching. He had never thought he'd be interested in the land, old wildcatter that he was, but time had proved him wrong.

"As long as he was around, I never could figure out why Southworth loved those steer so much," he mused. "Now I understand, all right. It isn't as profitable as oil...but it—I don't know how to put it—it gives you a good feeling inside."

Sue Ellen had brought up the cattle auction with a purpose. As J.R.'s wife, she felt it was her responsibility to promote his interests inside as well as outside the family. After all, someday, Southfork, Ewing Oil, and all the other Ewing possessions would be passed down, and she intended to see that she and J.R. got the lion's share of them.

"It'd be wonderful if you could share that feeling with your boys," she said pointedly.

Jock smiled. "I'd sure like to," he said, "but Bobby's on his way out of town to that junket in Las Vegas..."

Pam was suddenly alert. Bobby hadn't said anything to her about going to Las Vegas! Was he hiding it from her for a reason? Every inch of her body went taut with suspicion as she searched Bobby's eyes for an answer to her question. Bobby winced. He had been caught and he knew it. He looked at her pleadingly, as if to say, "I can't tell you about it right now, but trust me." Pam wondered if she could. If Bobby was keeping things from her already, in the first year of their marriage...

"...and J.R. never did give a hoot about cattle ranching," Jock finished with a shrug, as he picked up his second drink from its hiding place.

Ellie smiled as another memory flooded into her consciousness. "Of all my boys, Gary was the one who was the cowboy. He was the one who cared for the ranch...the only one who cared as much as I do."

Everyone around the pool fell silent. Mentioning Gary's name was like calling up a ghost. For sixteen years he had not been seen or heard from, and the circumstances of his departure were a painful memory, not only for Miss Ellie, but for Lucy as well.

Holding back her anger, Lucy said wryly, "My! How silent we all become as soon as my father's name is brought up! I wonder why that could be?"

J.R. got up from his chaise, affecting boredom.

His role in his brother's departure was something he wanted kept quiet, and any conversation about Gary made him fidgety. He strode over to the pool, about to dive in to wash away his discomfort, when he heard Sue Ellen say, "I feel certain that J.R. is just itching to go with you to that auction, Daddy."

So that was what she'd been after, J.R. thought. She knew damn well that he hated cows and ranching and everything connected with the land. His true love was oil, Ewing Oil in particular, and Sue Ellen knew it. J.R. was furious. His wife had the most underhanded and subtle way of digging a knife into him. Stowing his anger away for later, he dived into the pool, surfacing just in time to hear his father say, "Well, why the hell not, he'd be more than welcome to join me."

Sue Ellen walked over to the edge of the pool. "I have good news, my love. I've arranged everything. You and your daddy are going to the auction together tomorrow. Aren't you thrilled? Just think what a good time you'll have!"

He would have liked to pull her into the pool and hold her down till she was within an inch of drowning, but she turned on her heels and walked away from him, wiggling her luscious torso behind her. As she went, she passed Raoul carrying a second tray of drinks and, taking another one from his tray, she proceeded on toward the house.

"Sue Ellen!"

J.R.'s voice stopped Sue Ellen in her tracks as she approached the side door. "Yes, my sweet? Did you call me?" she said, in her silkiest tone.

"I'd like to know what you think you were doing back there." The look in J.R.'s eyes was enough to burn through steel, but Sue Ellen stood her ground. She was in the right, and she knew it.

"You know as well as I do that my duty as a wife is to aid and support my husband's cause," she replied with an air of combined innocence and rectitude. As she turned to go, J.R. grabbed her arm with a vise-like grip.

"What does my cause, as you put it, have to do with me going to that stupid auction?" he whispered.

Sue Ellen smiled at her husband's unaccustomed simplicity. "Jock is going," she smiled back at him. "Don't you think his first-born son ought to be by his side...for once in his life?"

"Not in a roomful of cows, I don't."

Sue Ellen's face grew stern. "Where you are is not important," she admonished him. Again she turned and started for the house. This time, J.R. did not grab her arm but, instead, took a moment to consider what she'd just said, and then followed her. He caught up to her at the door. She had to be put in her place.

"Let me tell you something, Sue Ellen..."

She wheeled on him. Her face was white with fury. "No. Let me tell *you* something. You may not be aware of what's happening, but I am. Your baby brother Bobby is slowly but surely usurping your place. If you don't watch out you'll lose everything."

J.R. was taken aback by the force of her outburst. "Nothing has been lost, Sue Ellen," he protested.

"Yes it has. I see that Bobby's in Ewing Oil now. That's something new. And what's more, your mama and daddy have let that girl into the family. If she's not a threat, I don't know who is."

It used to be that Sue Ellen was the golden girl of

the Ewing family. Time was when Jock and Miss Ellie hung on her every word. If only she'd had a child! She knew now that that was what they'd been waiting for all this time. It wasn't her fault, she knew that instinctively. But J.R. had never been willing to go for a checkup. She had finally reached the point of despair, and then Bobby had gone and married that Barnes girl who had the luck to get pregnant right away. Sue Ellen had watched and withered as the Barnes girl had stolen her spotlight in the family.

"Ever since she lost her baby, they've gone out of their way to be nice to her. They won't even listen to the little jokes you used to make about her anymore," Sue Ellen said. Her eyes glowed with hatred of her sister-in-law. That Barnes girl wasn't going to usurp her place in the family without a fight.

"That's just for the moment," J.R. retorted. "They have pity for her...because of the baby."

"Maybe. But little by little, I see you being dislodged. If you're not prepared to fight for yourself and for us, I am."

J.R. looked at the woman he had married and shook his head in admiration. She was everything he had hoped she'd be—his helpmate, his partner, his defender. She was right, and no matter how much he tried to reassure himself things were fine, he knew in his heart they weren't. As Sue Ellen walked into the house and up the stairs, J.R. followed her with his eyes. Something had to be done, and soon.

As they mounted the stairs on the way to their bedroom, Pamela Barnes Ewing looked up at her husband's strong, naked back and wondered if she hadn't made a terrible mistake. She had thrown away so much to marry him—her father's love, her brother's respect, her whole past. Had she thrown it away for nothing? Bobby had seemed so honest, so giving—was it all a lie? Was he just like all the other Ewings, as her father had told her so often? She had been so sure of him. But now, he was hiding things from her. This 'junket' to Las Vegas—why hadn't he told her about it? She thought of Sue Ellen and her marriage to J.R. It was all so sickening to her the way they manipulated each other. But as she followed Bobby upstairs, she wondered whether the same things were beginning to happen in her marriage.

Entering the bedroom behind him, she shut the door and, leaning against it with all her weight, she asked him, "Well, Bobby?"

Bobby turned around to face her. His strong, handsome face wore a quizzical expression. "Well?" He cocked his head and smiled a little half smile. If he was trying to disarm her, Pam thought, it wouldn't work.

"How about an explanation. What was all that about an oilmen's junket?" She searched his eyes for the answer to her hidden question: Bobby, are you hiding something from me? She found nothing there, though, only a blank stare.

"It's in Las Vegas. Tomorrow."

"And what you're telling me is that you're going." Pam wondered if Bobby noticed her lower lip trembling. But the answer she got was one she hadn't expected.

"Yes. And so are you. I had planned to tell you this afternoon. I thought it might be a nice surprise."

In her great relief, she ignored the hesitation in his voice. It was a dream come true. Not only was he still Bobby, her Bobby, but she would finally be getting away from Southfork for a few days. Able to breathe again! Able to relax without looking over her shoulder! It could have been Las Vegas; it could have been Death Valley, *anywhere*, as long as it wasn't Southfork!

Now she saw that he was waiting for her to say something. He was obviously feeling guilty for not telling her sooner and was sorry she'd been put through the hurt of hearing it from someone else. "Oh, honey..." she said, coming toward him, her arms open to him. But instead of returning her embrace, he backed away, almost as if he expected her to hit him.

"I remember my promise, h w I said I'd never go on the road anymore," he apologized.

Pam laughed and threw her grateful arms around his strong neck. She kissed him lightly on the lips and laughed softly. "You're sure it's all right?" asked Bobby, surprised at her reaction.

"Yes! Oh, Bobby, life on this ranch is driving me crazy!" She laughed playfully and hugged him again. He stroked her beautiful auburn hair.

"You're not accustomed to the life of leisure," he nodded.

Bobby drew away from her and looked straight into her eyes as if to make doubly sure she was telling him the truth. "So are we square? About everything?"

"We can start packing right now," she answered. She saw his accustomed self-confidence return, the color flowing into his face as he gazed into her eyes.

"I knew you'd forgive me for breaking my promise," he said, smiling. He kissed her lightly on the lips.

"On second thought," said Pamela, "let's not start packing just yet." And, taking him by the hand, she led him toward the bed.

Chapter Two

Las Vegas is a great leveler. On any given day, the city plays host to housewives from Michigan, retirees from Florida and New Mexico, underworld types from New York, all mixed in with a liberal dose of foreigners from all over the world. But on this day in Las Vegas, with all the cowboy hats and backslapping, the whole city seemed to be a plush gambling den deep in the heart of Texas. Everywhere there were hoots of triumph and long, drawled moans of despair from the gaming tables. The high rollers were in town, and the money was flowing fast and loose in all directions. When the oilmen hit Vegas, they gambled from dawn to dusk.

The oilmen's junket was a big one, and the hotel had graciously set aside an entire gaming floor just for the conventioneers. They all wore little derrick-shaped name tags on their chests, but the tags weren't really necessary. Their ease of manner, and something in their stance, identified them from a mile away.

At noon, the oilmen were invited to a special cocktail party in the gigantic suite of their host, Bobby Ewing. The floor-to-ceiling windows of the elegant suite looked out on the tacky strip. In a few hours, the neon lights of the casinos would transform the sight into a blaze of rainbow colors. But all the noise was coming from inside, where, their morning of gambling at an end, the oilmen were telling each other their stories of glory or defeat. Now they had their women by their sides. Most of the women were no more than half the age of the men. It was clear to even the most casual observer that at this gathering the non-wives far outnumbered the wives.

Bobby Ewing did not fit the usual definition of an oilman. He could gamble with the best of them, and he got along with almost everybody, but he was a family man now, and a loyal one. The tallest man in the room, Bobby stood in the far corner greeting his guests and their assorted wives or girlfriends, tactful enough not to say anything untoward about the latter, while remembering all the names and histories of the former.

Bobby was trading oil stories with Jordon Lee and Andy Bradley, members of the cartel, and old friends of the Ewing clan. He was shaking hands with total strangers, making new friends who might come in handy at some future date. A more charming host could not be imagined. That's why Jock Ewing had chosen Bobby over his eldest son, J.R., for the task of being the family diplomat. J.R. had made too many enemies in his short tenure as head of Ewing Oil. He made a profit for the company, all right, but Jock knew the enemies would come back to haunt J.R. down the line.

Jock had insisted that J.R. make room for Bobby in the company. The eldest son had fought like a bantam rooster, but Jock was still in charge, retired or not, and what he said went. Bobby became the company diplomat and fence-mender and, therefore, the one to go to Las Vegas to cement friendships and bury hatchets with the rest of the Texas oil community.

Bobby was pumping hands right and left, and at the same time carrying on a spirited conversation with a middle-aged oilman named Victor McLean and his equally middle-aged wife, Joan.

"You don't mean to tell me Jock Ewing would pass up one of these junkets," said Victor, shaking his head. For thirty-odd years Jock had never missed an oilmen's junket, and most of the men had no more than a passing acquaintance with his son. Jock was a colorful figure, and most of those present missed his high spirits. Bobby had a big pair of shoes to fill.

"I wouldn't lie to you, Victor," Bobby laughed easily. "He's a fanatical rancher these days. The cattle have won his old oilman's heart."

Victor raised his eyebrows in disbelief. For years Jock Ewing had had nothing but disdain for ranching. As far back as Texas history went, oilmen and ranchers had been on opposite sides of the fence, and there was never any love lost between them. In fact, Jock and old man Southworth, Miss Ellie's father, had had their problems almost from day one because of that very issue. Jock Ewing becoming a rancher was about as hard to believe as Ronald Reagan becoming a liberal.

"You positive it's Jock Ewing we're discussing?" said Victor.

"Positive," laughed Bobby. He was about to continue the conversation when there was a sudden commotion from the bedroom door. In between the dozen or so male figures surrounding her, Bobby could make out Pam, looking dazzling in her party dress, and trying her best to tactfully fend off the many advances coming at her. From all over the room, men began making a bee-line for her, leaving their unhappy wives and mistresses behind.

From his perch across the room, Bobby could make out snatches of the remarks being directed at his wife. A fat man was saying, "You're my blind date, I just know it!" while from the lips of a balding guest came the flattering, "I have always said, and I'll say it again—Bobby Ewing's parties attract only the best people." Pam's corner of the room buzzed with the agreement of several male guests.

"Bobby Ewing?" said Pam, playing along. "Never head of him. I must have wandered into the wrong room." But she continued walking as best as she could in his direction.

"Any room you walk into, little flower, is the right room for me," said a witty, would-be Lothario.

Pamela smiled, rolling her eyes. This was getting to be a bit too much. As she moved toward Bobby, she tossed back over her shoulder, "I'll check my calendar."

"Hell, I'll buy you a dozen calendars!" came the reply. As Pam reached Bobby, they looked at each other with loving amusement. They really were having a good time, the best they'd had in a long while.

"I'll say it again, Bobby Ewing's parties attract only the best people," repeated the bald suitor.

Bobby put his arm around Pam, and, loudly enough for the whole room to hear, he said, "You know, you're absolutely right. Nobody's better people than my wife!" There was a moment of stunned silence, and then everyone burst into genuine, heartfelt laughter.

J.R. Ewing felt like doing anything but laughing. He was having an awful time. Being at a cattle auction was not his idea of a good time at all. He couldn't see anything attractive about the stupid beasts. In fact, they reminded him more than anything of ugly women. Besides, they smelled like hell and, were dirty, too, no matter how much they were scrubbed for auction. Why people would devote their lives to these beasts, love them like family, and pay outrageous prices for them, was beyond him. But much as he would have liked to kill Sue Ellen for volunteering him to go, he knew it was important for him to maintain a close relationship with his father if he expected to retain complete control of Ewing Oil.

Even so, it was all he could do to keep his good humor, what with Lucy and Ray Krebbs along. As far as J.R. could see, Ray and Jock were much too close; more like father and son than employer and employee. Ray Krebbs had his nerve, J.R. thought indignantly. Even though J.R. went out carousing with Ray—drinking and meeting women—there was no need for him to get so buddy-buddy with Jock.

As for Lucy, he could barely stand to be in the same room with her for meals every day, let alone go traveling with her. In all her 16 years she had been nothing but trouble, not only to him, but to everyone in the family. Not that he was sorry he'd driven her mother and father away. One was a drunk and the other a tramp, and no matter how much he hated Lucy, she was still a Ewing. Better for her to be raised at Southfork, no matter how trying she was, than for her to be raised by that no-account mother of hers. God knows what she would have become. Why, she'd been given the best of everything, and look how badly she'd turned out.

As they walked past stall after stall, the one bunch of cows exactly the same as every other, with the same smell and the same flies, J.R. began to wish he'd stayed home at Southfork, even if it did mean sacrificing some of his daddy's good will. After all, there were other ways to win the old man's heart, and Jock hadn't been expecting J.R. to come along anyway. As if the stench weren't bad enough, his feet began to hurt him.

He had worn his fancy Western boots, as he did every day, but this was a new pair. Now, at noon, his shirt was sticking to his chest, and his feet ached from all the unaccustomed walking he'd been doing. In the course of a normal day, he'd have been either behind his desk or behind the wheel of *Ewing 3*, his flashy Mercedes. Either way, he'd have been sitting down. He knew the walking was good for him, and that it would help reduce the roll in his middle. Nevertheless, he wished he'd stayed home.

He noticed that Lucy kept looking at her watch

28

as they walked along. He wondered if she was as bored as he was. Much as they didn't get along, J.R. felt sure cattle auctions weren't her cup of tea any more than they were his. He wondered why she'd agreed to come. Nobody'd pressured her—she'd volunteered. Now she looked up at Jock and said, batting her baby blue eyes at him, "Grandpa, could I go take a look at the Western store they've got here?"

That did it. J.R. had taken enough. He was just ready to sit down and take a load off his feet, and now they'd have to wait for that numbskull niece of his to do her shopping. "Isn't it about time we had lunch?" he complained.

Lucy looked up at her uncle and smiled her sweetest smile. "I don't want any lunch," she said. Once again, she turned her eyes to Jock hopefully.

"Well, why not," said the old man indulgently.

J.R. snorted. His father was getting old, that was for sure. First Bobby, now Lucy—it seemed that everyone had the old man wrapped around their little finger—everyone except him. "*I'm* hungry," he interjected.

Without waiting for a reply from Jock, Lucy took advantage of her momentary freedom. "Thanks, Grandpa. I'll only be gone an hour. I'll meet you right here..." And with that, she started to run off in the direction of the exit.

"Lucy!" Jock Ewing's powerful voice boomed out through the hall. Lucy stopped in her tracks, as if she'd been caught in some illegal act, and turned around. She started back toward her grandfather with her eyes cast down and her hands clasped behind her back. Jock eyed her sternly.

"Yes, Grandpa?" she asked, her voice affecting innocence.

"What happens if you see something you want?"

"Huh?" His question had taken her by complete surprise. Was he accusing her of something? What did he mean? Was he testing her? Trying to trip her up?

"When you get to the Western store... What are you going to do without any money if you want to buy something?"

Lucy breathed a sigh of relief. "Oh. Oh, right..." she muttered, coming forward with as big a smile as she could muster. She wondered if her cheeks were as flushed as they felt.

Jock smiled at his pretty granddaughter. So like a Ewing, he thought. So impatient to get where she was going she forgot to ask for money to buy something once she got there. He reached into his pocket and pulled out the wad of large bills he always carried with him. Jock Ewing was a man who believed in carrying large amounts of cash. Wetting his fingers with his tongue, he peeled off a few bills and handed them, not to Lucy, but to Ray. "Tag along with her, would you, Ray?" he said. Jock never was a man to trust a young lady with a lot of cash. Never could tell what sort of trouble she'd get into with it.

Lucy protested. "No, that's all right..." she began.

But J.R., as anxious to get rid of Ray as he was to get rid of Lucy, broke in saying, "You'd better go with her, Ray...there're some rough characters around here." Jock nodded in agreement. It was obvious the discussion was closed. With a troubled look, Lucy turned and walked away, with Ray following close behind her.

As soon as they were out of earshot, Lucy turned and, without breaking stride, said over her shoulder to Ray, "Leave me alone, Ray."

Ray was startled, but firm. When Jock gave an order, Ray followed it, no questions asked. It had been that way ever since he was 15, when Jock took him on as a ranch hand, broke and in trouble. Ray had been grateful then, and he had never had cause to regret his gratitude. "You heard what Jock said," he said sternly.

Lucy pursed her lips with determination. She was going to have to take drastic measures.

"I heard what he said, but I'm going alone. I'm going somewhere else, not to the store, and you're not coming with me."

Ray frowned. He had come to expect this sort of behavior from Lucy. She was always getting in trouble and hiding it from the family. But it surprised him that she was evading him. They had always been close friends, and she had confided in him more than once. Apparently, whatever was happening now was too secret and sensitive to include him.

"Are you going to tell me where you're off to?" he asked, not a little hurt at being left out of her confidence.

Lucy's attention was elsewhere. At another time, Ray's feelings might have meant a lot to her, but there was too much at stake at this particular moment. She glanced at her watch. She was two minutes late, and she was still a hundred yards from the appointed spot.

"Beat it!' she cried, and broke into a run.

Ray followed a few steps behind. "I can't!" he shouted.

Finally he caught up with her at the meeting place, but her party had not yet arrived. She glanced down the street to see if he was coming, then she glanced at Ray. It was obvious to Lucy that she was going to have to say or do something right away—something drastic.

Looking Ray right in the eye, she blurted out, "If you don't get away from me, I'll tell Granddaddy all those secrets you told me."

Ray was stunned. Long ago, in a moment of intimacy, he had confided something, and she had promised never to tell. What was going on with her, he wondered, to make her threaten him like that. "You wouldn't," he said.

Lucy stared right back at him. "Try me."

"What's so important?" Ray asked, trying to reestablish some sort of rapport.

Just at that moment a car pulled up next to them. Lucy glanced at it nervously, then turned to Ray and said, "I'll be back in an hour. Meet me here."

Ray looked in at the driver of the car, and suddenly it all came together for him. The driver was Jimmy Monahan, Pamela's cousin, and a Barnes. So that was it! Lucy saw the look in Ray's eyes. "I know what you're thinking, and you're wrong. Not that I care."

Ray shook his head skeptically. "Bobby's bringing home Digger Barnes' daughter is enough," he said. "Jock's not going to stand for you going out with Digger's nephew."

Lucy drew herself up to her full diminutive height and looked right up into Ray's eyes. "Well, then, just as well you don't tell him anything about it. Right, Ray?" And with a flourish, she got into the car and slammed the door behind her.

As the car pulled away, Ray stared after it sadly. He couldn't help but feel a sense of foreboding. Nothing good could come of this, he thought to himself, but a lot of bad sure could.

At the Ewing suite, the party had begun to thin out as the guests departed for another gambling session, or, in some cases, for an afternoon of passion behind closed doors. Catching Pamela between good-byes, Bobby took her aside and said, "The rest of these folks don't seem so anxious to leave. I'll tell you what—why don't you go on down, and I'll meet you at the pool as soon as I can."

Pam smiled. Bobby was so sensitive, so on the lookout for every signal of her feelings. He knew before she said a word that she was tired of all the socializing, that she longed for some time alone with him, away from Southfork, away from oilmen, just the two of them. She was about to head for the bedroom and change into her swimsuit when a six-foot-tall redhead in a shimmering gold dress snaked her way over to Bobby, smiling tipsily from ear to ear. "Bobby Ewing!" she simpered, her enormous breasts heaving under her low-cut, skin-tight dress, "I'm so glad you found your way back to this hotel. It's been so boring here without you!" And, kissing Bobby square and long on the lips before he knew what was happening, the red-haired vixen continued on her way to the bar.

Wiping the lipstick from his mouth and

smiling sheepishly, Bobby turned toward Pam and shrugged his shoulders. She knew all about his wild days. Smiling innocently, Pam sidled up to him and slipped her arm inside his. "My place is with my husband—at all times," she said coyly, and they both burst out laughing.

Pete's was an old-fashioned diner housed in a former railroad car. Red plastic booths and formica tables lined one side, a matching formica counter the other. Pete, himself, an enormously fat but obviously good-natured fellow, leaned behind the cash register counting the receipts from lunch. It had been busy for a while, but now the place was virtually empty. At the far end of the diner, Valene Clements bussed the remaining dishes. The waitress' blonde hair was held back with bobby pins to keep it out of her face. But even with the beads of sweat that marked her brow, Valene was a pretty woman. She had seen younger days, but with a little rest, a little make-up, and a little happiness, she would be quite a sight to see.

At the counter, the last customer threw down a few coins and turned to go. Valene took his plate as she passed and scooped up the meager tip. "Thanks," she said to the customer's back as he approached the door. He turned around to see if she was being sarcastic. But by the time he turned around, she'd covered up her disappointment, turning her smirk into her brightest smile. No point in alienating the customers. Cheap as they might be, they were still her bread and butter.

Coming out of the kitchen and wiping her hands on a rag, Valene could see a car pulling into the lot. Out of the door popped Lucy Ewing with

Jimmy Monahan trailing after her. As Lucy came through the door of the diner, Valene smiled from the bottom of her heart, for the first time in days.

"Hi!" said Lucy brightly.

"Hi."

Lucy walked over to the counter and plopped down on one of the stools. As Jimmy came over to sit by her, Lucy pointed to him and said, "You know Jimmy Monahan, don't you?"

Valene nodded at the boy. He was handsome, all right, and obviously in love with Lucy. "Course I do. From the last time. How are you Jimmy?"

"Fine," said the boy, obviously happy to be spoken to cordially. Lucy had hardly given him the time of day all the way there. "How 'bout you? How you doing?"

"Just fine, thanks," lied Val, and turning to Lucy, she said, "Just give me a chance to clear these dishes up, and I'll be right back. We can take a walk..." With that, Valene began putting the finishing touches on the lunch hour as expertly and quickly as only a life-long waitress can do.

Jimmy picked up the plastic-covered menu and began to look it over. Pete, seeing that Lucy was preoccupied, turned to the young man and began a conversation. "They look the same age, don't they—just like two sisters."

Jimmy looked up. "Huh?" he asked.

"Those two," said Pete. "They look the same age. You'd never guess they were mama and daughter."

"Uh-huh," Jimmy said expressionlessly. He put down the menu and, with a sigh of frustration said, "Grilled cheese."

***

Finally the party was over. Bobby, still looking remarkably fresh and well-groomed, shook hands with the last of the guests and smiled one more smile. "Be seeing you at the tables, then, Jack."

Jack nodded and let go of Bobby's hand. "Right," he said. "I'll be the one who's crying in his drink!"

They both laughed, Bobby dutifully, Jack with genuine hilarity at his own humor, and Bobby closed the door behind him. He took a deep breath and blew it out, turning to Pam, who was collapsed in a chair. "Ready for a swim?" she said. They both nodded. No other words were necessary.

Pam dragged herself out of her chair, and began to unbutton her dress. She was about to pull it off completely when there was a knock at the door. Husband and wife looked at each other with pained expressions on their faces. "Another old acquaintance," moaned Pamela.

Bobby went over and took his lovely wife by the shoulders. Kissing her lightly on the lips, he whispered, "I'll say hello and send him on his way." There was another knock at the door. "Hang on a minute," shouted Bobby over his shoulder, and, with another kiss for Pamela, he turned and made for the door. Quickly, Pam grabbed her bathing suit from a drawer and made her way to the bedroom. The bedroom door shut just as Bobby opened the door of the suite. Outside stood not another good old boy, but a bellboy, dressed in the green uniform and gold-embroidered cap of the hotel staff.

"Yes?" said Bobby, puzzled.

"I'm here to clean up the place," said the bellboy, and without another word, dashed past

Bobby into the room and began to gather up the empty glasses and used napkins.

"Hold on a minute!" cried Bobby. "The lady and I are on our way to the pool."

But instead of stopping and doing as Bobby had asked, the bellboy continued with what he was doing, his back to Bobby, saying only, "Don't forget your suntan oil."

Bobby was beginning to get annoyed. Even for the good-natured fellow he was, there was a limit to how much he could take. Maintaining his politeness, and raising his voice only a little, he said, "What I mean to say is...why don't you wait till we leave to clean up?"

The bellboy shook his head. Without pausing in what he was doing, he chirped. "I couldn't bear to let this room stay messy. I have to have things neat and clean or it drives me crazy."

What was wrong with this guy, wondered Bobby? Was he a neat nut, or a maniac, or what? Now, upon closer scrutiny, Bobby noticed that the man wasn't really cleaning up the mess, but only rearranging it, taking things from one part of the room and depositing them in another. What's more, Bobby realized that the man was keeping his back to him at all times. Anger welled up in Bobby. He didn't like being toyed with. "Now, just a damned minute—" he began, but the bellboy cut him off.

"Sorry...I've already started. Can't stop now."

Now Bobby had had enough. He strode over to the fellow and, grabbing him by the arm, spun him around so he could look him in the eye. "All right, mister. Now hear this—"

Bobby stopped dead in mid-sentence. The man

was smiling at him—beaming! And he looked familiar, too...the blonde hair, the craggily handsome face, the dancing eyes... Bobby couldn't believe his eyes! "Gary?" he asked, just to make double-sure.

The bellboy nodded, his smile growing even wider. "In person."

Bobby shook his head in disbelief. "Gary..." And then, extending his hand, "Well, son of a gun..." Now he realized that a handshake was woefully inadequate to the moment. He pulled Gary to him, and they embraced, tightly, slapping each other on the back, swaying from side to side.

At that moment, Pam, wearing a swimsuit and a loose robe, opened the bedroom door. She looked incredulously at her husband and the bellboy acting like old pals.

Bobby turned and saw her. Both he and the bellboy were beaming. "Honey—I'd like you to meet Gary."

Pam nodded, thinking that, in spite of the uniform, this must be another good old boy oilman, one with a sense of humor, and one Bobby was somewhat closer with than the others. She walked toward him, hand outstretched to shake his, as she'd shaken so many others that day.

Bobby saw the mistake she was making and interjected, "No, Pammy. This is Gary."

Pam still didn't quite get it—she stopped in her tracks and furrowed her brows, searching for recognition. Bobby helped her.

"Gary Ewing—my brother."

Chapter Three

As they sat under the shade of a big weeping willow on one of the run-down benches that lined the park across the way from Pete's, Lucy and her mother stared into one another's eyes. They tried with all the energy that was in them to get inside each other's souls, to recapture the time together that was so irretrievably lost forever. They really did look like sisters, with their identical shades of blonde hair, their aquiline noses and full, sensual lips. Even the bright twinkle in their eyes was the same. Their true relationship was disguised only by the narrow difference in their ages, which made them look like sisters rather than mother and daughter. Valene was only thirty-two to Lucy's sixteen, testimony to the storm her marriage and pregnancy had provoked among her husband's family.

As they sat together, shaded from the intense heat of the Texas summer afternoon, Lucy begged her mother to tell her again the romantic story of her mother's first meeting with her father. The story somehow seemed to stir something in Lucy, as if she were hearing her own story for the first time.

Seventeen years earlier, Valene had been working as a waitress in another restaurant—one where the prices were much higher than Pete's but the atmosphere not nearly as congenial—quite sleazy, in fact. Young Valene had had to wear skimpy uniforms and flirt with the customers, whether she liked them or not. She almost always didn't. They tended to be the kind of men who thought of a woman merely as an object for pleasing their every desire. Regularly, the pretty young waitress would be bothered and teased by the late-night patrons, and occasionally she would even be manhandled by a customer who had consumed more than his share of firewater. It was all Valene could do to fight off these advances. The management gave her no help at all. As far as they were concerned, the customer was always right, and if the help couldn't play by those rules, they could seek employment elsewhere.

It was on one of those Saturday nights, at about two in the morning, when she'd first met Gary Ewing. She was just about to pack it in and go upstairs to change, when she was set upon by a couple of big, burly customers, one of whom grabbed her and announced his intention to bring her outside to his car. The other patrons ignored her cries for help; in fact, they seemed rather amused. All but one. A blonde cowboy got up from his table in the corner and interceded on her behalf. While he was a tall man, he wasn't nearly as powerfully built as her two tormentors, but he wasn't nearly as drunk either. It didn't come down to a fight, after all. Perhaps the two low-lifes could sense that they were too drunk to make a fight of it. Perhaps, like most bullies, they were cowards when faced with somebody remotely close to their own size. In any case they'd left the establishment, abandoning the field to her unknown protector. She hadn't had time till that moment to notice how handsome he was.

"I was a fifteen-year-old girl...just a kid..." Valene trailed off.

She was half lost in her memories, but Lucy interrupted her reverie. Her own interest was overflowing, and she felt compelled to hear more. "But you lied about your age to get the job," she prodded.

Valene smiled wistfully, and looked again at the beautiful girl she and Gary had produced. If only he could see her now—he would be so proud. But that would never happen, she knew. Even so, she was grateful to have Lucy back in her life. That in itself was a miracle she'd never expected to have happen.

"Yep," she answered. "There he stood... handsomest feller I ever laid eyes on...and he put me in a chair and stared at me for a long while..." Valene shook herself out of it. "You sure you're not tired of hearing this story?"

Lucy nodded emphatically. "Uh-huh," she coached. "And then you asked him what he wanted to order."

Valene laughed and picked up where Lucy had left off. "And he answered: 'I'm not sure; what does a man in love drink when he's thirsty?' I knew he was only flirting...but it was the best kind of flirting." In her hard, sad fifteen years, she'd rarely been treated to that kind of warm, friendly attention. "He gave me the feeling of...of being a lady...of being somebody..."

Lucy nodded as if she remembered it, too, as if it were a part of her own past she was remembering, instead of a love story she'd come by secondhand, one that had happened before she'd even been born. "And that's how you felt with him all the time," she sighed.

"All the time," Val agreed. And then her face clouded over as she remembered more of the story. "For a while, anyway..." For a moment, Val was lost in thought; then she looked at her watch. She was testing the limits of Pete's good graces, she knew, and she was also aware that Lucy had a timetable to meet. "We'd best be getting back," she said, getting up from the bench and stretching her body, already weary from just half a day's work.

Lucy rose, too, and the two of them, hand in hand, began walking back toward the diner. The movement made Val feel brighter, more alert and hopeful. She continued her story, winding it up quickly. "Every night when I got off work, he was there to walk me home."

Lucy broke in again, sharing the memory, making it more fully her own. "And when you got to your front door...'Miss Valene,' he said, 'I feel compelled by some inner need to ask you to marry me.'"

"And you said...?" asked Lucy, as if she didn't already know.

"Not a word," her mother answered. "What was I gonna say? But he understood my silence to mean yes. And just three days after that we were married. We never touched each other till after. Your father was a genuine gentleman. It was lucky he was, too, 'cause I would've been terrified if he wasn't. I was a kid, just a little kid, really." It was no more than the truth. At fifteen, she'd still been a virgin, in spite of her hard youth and her sleazy place of employment. "The times we spent together..."

"...were here and gone." Lucy finished her sentence for her.

Valene went on as if she hadn't been interrupted. "He was the dearest man I ever knew, Till he brought me home to Southfork to meet his folks." Valene's face darkened at the memory.

"He kept refusing to take me home," Val remembered, "putting me off...but after I got pregnant with you, honey, I made him bring me home to meet the family."

Lucy knew this story by heart. She remembered all the details.

Because of the family's reaction and Val's fear of J.R., she had decided to run away with her baby to someplace they would never find her. It was a desperate move, but Valene hadn't counted on her brother-in-law's cunning. He'd tracked her down to her mother's house and sent a couple of "good old boys" after her to take Lucy from her. She had begged her mother to help her, to hide the baby for her and take care of Lucy for a while. But her mother, who had always been a selfish woman, was busy romancing a man she hoped would help her career and had no place in her life for a baby, let alone for her own daughter. She'd left Valene and the baby at the mercy of

J.R.'s thugs. They'd taken Lucy from her and warned her never to show her face at Southfork again. In fact, they let her know in no uncertain terms, that it would be best for her health if she left the state altogether. She hadn't been able to bring herself to go that far, but her terror had kept her away from Southfork and her daughter for sixteen years.

"I used to believe I despised J.R. Ewing more than anybody ever despised anybody," she said out loud. "But I was wrong. I hate him now even more than I hated him then." She put her arm around her daughter, and they continued back to the restaurant.

Bobby, Pam and Gary sat closely huddled around the table. When the waitress arrived, Bobby began to order drinks for each of them.

"No, Bobby, just a club soda for me," Gary said.

Bobby looked at him in surprise, then complied with his wishes.

Gary began his story—the long, sixteen-year saga of his lonely, tragic, fugitive existence. The experience with Valene and his family's reaction to her had been traumatic, and Gary, always weak of will, had begun to drink heavily. By the time he ran away from Southfork, he was well on his way to the depths of degradation. The shame of abandoning his helpless wife and child to his wolf of a brother and his unbending father had made him into a full-fledged alcoholic.

Although his father had immediately cut him off without a dime to his name, Gary had started out with quite a bundle. But along with his alcoholism, he also had a weak spot for gambling, and the two monsters together had pushed him into ruination. Now, as he sat with his brother, who had been just a kid when all this had happened, and with his brother's lovely wife, who was free of all blame for his expulsion, he unburdened himself freely and fully, his natural good humor and friendliness masking the sense of tragedy that clouded his existence every day of his life.

For Bobby, it was a dream come true. There was nothing more important to him than to see his family come together again. Having been only a boy at the time, he was unaware of J.R.'s sinister role in Gary's departure, and he probably wouldn't have believed it anyway. Pam, on the other hand, knew first-hand what it felt like to incur the wrath of Jock Ewing and his boy, J.R. She looked at her brother-in-law and could readily imagine everything he had been through. After all, she had been through quite a lot herself and, like Gary, she too had lost a child because of the Ewings.

As they sat together bound by their shared associations and their troubled family lives, Gary continued his story. "Like I was telling you," he said, taking a sip of his club soda, "one day I looked at myself in the mirror, and there I was... seventy, eighty grand in the hole...an out-and-out alkie...no place to call home. So I did the thing any real man would do..." He stopped, waiting for a reaction from his audience. Bobby and Pam looked up at him quizzically.

"Which was?" Pam finally asked.

"Blacked out completely," Gary replied with a wry grin. "One morning, barely able to get out of bed, I looked in the mirror and realized I'd been beaten up badly. My face was just a mass of bruises. I don't have any idea who did it—though I'm sure I deserved it." He stopped for a moment, letting the bitterness of the memory come flooding back into his consciousness before continuing. "Sometime in the afternoon I found out it was two weeks later than I thought. I still don't know what happened to me during those two weeks."

Bobby took a long look at the brother he'd known only as a boy. Gary's pain was clear to him, and he felt his brother's agony fully. If only he'd been a grown man then and been able to help his brother. He shook his head in disbelief. "Holy Hannah," was all he could manage to say.

"You can say that again," said Gary, with his never-failing good humor. "In any case," he went on, "I thought about it, and it seemed to me that whoever'd busted my face into a pulp might be back. So I got the first bus out of town."

Pam looked long and hard at her new-found brother-in-law, whom she liked so much more than the brother-in-law she shared her home with. He was so different from J.R., and even from Bobby. He seemed to know first-hand, through his painful, lonely odyssey, what life without luxury was really all about. She, too, knew the pain of deprivation, though not nearly as well as Gary, and she felt herself deeply in sympathy with him and caring for his welfare.

"And that's how you found yourself here?" she asked, prodding him to go on with his story.

"In the end, yes," he answered.

Bobby looked at the club soda in his brother's hand. "And you've never taken a drink since then?'' he inquired.

"I'm afraid I have," said Gary, shaking his head sadly, "I kept kicking it, then falling back."

Pam thought of her poor father, Digger, and his long, failing battle with alcoholism. Maybe there was something she could learn from Gary's struggle which would help her father to finally lay the monster of drink to rest. "How'd you finally kick the habit?" she asked intently.

Gary smiled his broadest smile since he'd come in the door and revealed himself to them. "Got work tending bar!" he said proudly.

Bobby and Pam were shocked. It was the last thing they expected him to say. "You're kidding!" Bobby blurted out, smiling but flabbergasted nevertheless.

Gary raised his index finger to his head. "It makes sense if you give it some thought," he said. "You keep looking at booze all day and night long. It really makes you face up to it."

Pam shook her head in admiration. The incredible courage it must have taken to face his demons day after day and never give in to them! It was amazing to her that the very same person could be so weak as to slip into the depths the way Gary had and, at the same time, be strong enough to lick it in the way he had. In her heart, she knew the answer to her next question, but she asked it anyway, just to make sure. "And what about the compulsion to gamble. What did you do about that one?"

Gary smiled at her. He had known her only for an hour, yet he felt sure of her good heart, and of her goodwill towards him. He liked her enormously, and what's more, he trusted her. "What do you think?" he said. "I came to Las Vegas and got hired as a croupier in the casino."

Pam and Bobby looked at each other, and then they both burst out laughing. Gary, too, felt the laughter coming over him. It was a laughter of enjoyment and appreciation, and of irony, too.

"I can't believe it!" Bobby gasped.

Pam couldn't repress her amazement any longer. "You mean to tell me you really do work here?" she asked.

Gary nodded his head. "At the Emperor, not here. But I had heard that the Texas junket was here. I looked over the convention list in the lobby. I saw you listed for this room, so I borrowed this uniform and came on in." He laughed again, thinking how he had borrowed the bellboy's uniform for the occasion, and how silly he must have looked in it—a thirty-four year old man in an outsized uniform.

Bobby stopped laughing suddenly. A troubling thought had occurred to him. "What if you'd seen Daddy's name on that list?" He knew it was a difficult question, and he didn't want to inject any more pain into the happy occasion than had to be there, but he felt he couldn't rest until he knew the answer.

Gary was well aware of the seriousness of the question, and he fell silent for a long while, thinking, before he answered. "Maybe I'd have come up, maybe not," he finally said. It was impossible for him to be certain. He had been through enough to know that a person never really knows how he's going to behave until the actual situation is before him.

Bobby wasn't through yet. There was another

question to be asked. "J.R.?" he said, his eyes searching his brother's.

Again, Gary fell silent. As hard as it had been for him to answer Bobby's last question, this one was a lot harder. All the anger, and the terror, and the pain, came back to him in a rush of emotion. There was no answer he could make. He stared into space without moving. Finally, Pam broke the deep silence in the room. "Gary," she said softly, grasping his tightly-clenched hand, "you and I have a lot in common."

Gary looked deeply into his sister-in-law's compassionate eyes, and smiled. Pam smiled back at him. Bobby, feeling the need to balance the scales, said, only half believing his words, "J.R. isn't *that* bad—is he?"

That broke the moment. All at once both Gary and Pam burst out laughing, as though it were the funniest thing Bobby had ever said. At first, Bobby felt hurt and defensive, as if they were laughing at him. But then, he understood. The need to laugh overcame him, too, and he joined his wife and his long-lost brother in hilarious release.

As they approached the steps of the diner, Lucy knew it was past time for her to be getting back to the auction. Ray was waiting. In spite of her threat, which she felt sorry she'd had to make, she knew she could not count on him if she stayed away much longer. Besides, she was wearing Jimmy Monahan's patience thin, she knew. She could see him looking angrily through the window at her. He had long since finished his sandwich. She knew she was using him, but she felt she had no choice. No matter what, she had to keep seeing her mother. It was the only thing that gave meaning to her life, and if she had to use people and threaten people to get to see Valene, she reasoned, so be it.

Feeling she had only another moment or two to spend with her mother, Lucy blurted out what was on her mind. "Mama," she pleaded, "why don't we find a place and move in together?"

Valene smiled lovingly at her brave, impetuous daughter. "Mmmm...wouldn't that be a dream?" But in her heart, she knew it was impossible. Nevertheless, Lucy went on pleading, hoping by persistence to overcome overwhelming odds.

"I bet we could rent a little apartment somewhere..." she ventured.

Valene shook her head sadly. "Darlin',"—she caressed her daughter's long blonde hair—"if J.R. Ewing had any idea we were even meeting like this he'd have me thrown out of the state in no time. Maybe he'd even do worse. Imagine what he'd do if you and I moved in together."

Lucy knew what her mother had said was true, but in her desperation, she groped for other, more extreme solutions to their unsolvable problem. "We could leave the state!" she cried.

Again, Valene found herself shaking her head. It was a gesture she'd had to repeat over and over again during her meetings with Lucy. She wanted to be together as much as Lucy did, but she knew from first-hand experience just how impossible it would be. "I left the state when you were just a newborn," she said, with a note of finality in her voice. "He tracked us down then. I'm sure as sure can be he'd track us down now."

Jimmy had paid his check and come outside, too

impatient to wait for her any longer. "I suppose he might," Lucy said, still trying to make some headway. "But listen, haven't I told you about Bobby's wife? She's Digger Barnes' daughter. And J.R. hasn't been able to do anything about it..." Her voice trailed off questioningly, and her eyes searched her mother's for any sign of hope. There was none to be found.

"He will, in time, darlin'," Valene said, with a bitter edge to her voice.

"But—" Lucy began, but Valene interrupted her, putting an end to all conversation on the subject.

"Let's just leave it like this for now, all right, honey? We'll talk about it again in time."

It wasn't much, but it was a crumb of hope. Lucy seized on it. "Whatever you say, mama," she said, smiling peacefully, and, reaching up, she kissed her mother tenderly on the cheek. Her eyes were misting over now, and it was all she could do to hold back the tears. "I'll see you again as soon as I can manage to get away," she whispered.

Valene nodded. She, too, was close to tears. "I'll be waiting for you honey," she said. "Take good care of yourself. Bye, Jimmy," she finished, as he came up beside them.

Without another word, Lucy turned and accompanied Jimmy to his car. Valene watched as they pulled out of the parking lot and turned into the street. Long after they were out of sight, she was still standing there, holding on to the last sweet echo of her dear, lost daughter.

Gary sat staring at the brother he'd known only as a child, wondering at the fine, strong handsome man he'd become in the intervening years. The conversation had drifted, covering many areas— the family, Dallas, Bobby's new role in the family business—and now, finally, they had gotten around to discussing the most important subject of all for Gary: his daughter. Gary sat, drinking in the words, trying to create a picture in his mind for himself of the girl he'd seen only as a newborn baby, the girl he'd so shamefully run off and abandoned all those years ago. It hurt him just to think of it, but it soothed the pain to hear Bobby describe her, the intimate details of the description making her more real to him than she ever could have been before.

"Lucy's still cheery and petite..." Bobby was telling him. Gary tried to make the baby's face in his mind grow into a young woman's face, but it was hard, too hard. "...with long, blonde hair and a smile that melts steel," Bobby went on, "and gentle..."

Pam had heard enough. What was Bobby trying to do? She could stay silent no longer. She felt she had to correct the picture Bobby was painting for his brother's benefit. "She's a wild Indian," she interjected, cutting Bobby's description off in mid-stream.

Bobby was shocked at his wife's depiction, and annoyed with her for spoiling the impression he was trying to convey. "Honey!" he complained.

His wife shook her head, and went on. "Sorry, Bobby, but that's not Lucy as I know her, and I've got to say so." She turned to Gary, and, seeing the puzzled expression on his face, she continued, by way of an explanation. "They all treat her like she's made of glass, which is miles from the truth.

She's got the Ewing rage. *And* the fighting spirit. *And* the willfulness. *And* the pride."

Bobby had heard enough. What his wife was saying might have been true, looked at from her point of view, but it wasn't exactly a fitting picture to paint for a father who'd been pining away for his daughter for sixteen years. "Hey, wait a minute, honey..." he tried to stop her.

But Gary, who'd been staring curiously at Pamela, cut in with words that surprised Bobby completely. "So far she sounds good," he said, smiling at Pam.

Pam nodded eagerly, first at Gary, then at her husband. Then, looking back at Gary, she said, "That's what I'm trying to say. Underneath it all, she's really likable."

"Do you like her, Pam?" Gary asked her pointedly. He had to know, and the best way of finding out was by asking a direct question of the only person in the family who would tell him the unvarnished truth, not trying to spare his feelings.

Pam smiled as she thought of her saucy niece, and of her spiteful behavior with the radio the day before. "She'd get mad at me for saying it, but I like her a whole lot."

Gary breathed a sigh of relief. "If you like her, Pam, I'm sure I would, too." He truly liked his new sister-in-law. She was a woman worthy of eminent trust, direct, good-hearted and unspoiled by life at Southfork. He felt that with Pamela around, Lucy was in good hands, no matter what other influences were working against her.

Suddenly, it occurred to Gary how long he'd been away from his post at the gaming tables. He glanced at his watch, and the time confirmed his fears. "I'd better get back to work," he said, apologetically. He would have liked to stay on and talk until the wee hours of the morning, but his job was still important to him, and he couldn't afford to lose it. Not just yet, anyway. He got up from the table, and Bobby and Pam rose with him. They walked to the door with their arms around each other, their love for each other a warm glow emanating from their closeness and radiating into all corners of the room.

At the door, Bobby grabbed his brother by both shoulders and spun him around to face him. "Can we treat you to dinner?" he asked.

Gary smiled. "I never turn down an offer like that," he answered. His life had taken an amazing turn for the better, and he wasn't about to let it go with just an hour's worth of conversation. There was so much more catching up to do! With an embrace for Bobby, and a warm kiss on the cheek for Pam, Gary wheeled and went out the door. Bobby and Pam watched him retreating down the hallway, his pace brisk, a bounce in his walk, and whistling a little tune to himself.

Closing the door to the suite, Bobby clapped his hands together and gave full vent to the happiness that was brimming over inside him. "Oh, wow!" he cried, smiling from ear to ear. Without another word, he walked eagerly across the room and picked up the telephone.

A wave of alarm swept over Pam. What was Bobby doing? With every ounce of her intuition, she knew, and she knew she had to stop him before he went on with it. "Who're you phoning, Bobby?" she asked, just to make sure.

Bobby lowered the receiver, turned to her, and

smiled incredulously as if she should have known. "Mama. Who do you think I'm phoning?" he shrugged. And, with that, he resumed dialing.

Without another moment's hesitation, Pam rushed to her husband and covered his dialing hand with hers, stopping him in mid-number. Taking the receiver from his other hand, she placed it back down in its cradle. "Don't. Not yet," she said simply. It was more of a warning than a plea.

Bobby was confused. Why was she stopping him? Why didn't she want him to share his wonderful news? "Why the heck not?" he shook his head in puzzlement.

Pam was astounded at her husband's lack of sensitivity. She wasn't mad at him—she knew it was just his naive enthusiasm that prevented him from understanding the conflicting emotions she sensed in Gary. Bobby saw only the genuine joy Gary had gotten from their meeting. He hadn't looked far enough to see that the joy was also a cover for fear—fear and tremendous anxiety.

She could see that she was going to have to be plain-spoken with Bobby if she was to make him understand the situation fully. "Aren't you assuming too much? Gary didn't say he wanted to go home," she spelled it out.

Bobby exhaled a short little one-note laugh of disbelief. "He came to see us, didn't he?" It seemed perfectly obvious to Bobby — if Gary had looked him up, it was because he was ready to end his long exile and come home where he belonged.

Pam stuck to her guns. "That doesn't mean he's ready to see the whole family," she said. She thought of the oppressive atmosphere at Southfork, and of Gary's sensitive nature, which was apparent to her even after only an hour's conversation. She was seeing Gary with the eyes of her heart, as clearly as she had ever seen anything in her life. But to Bobby, the evidence of his eyes overwhelmed any other points of view.

"You saw him yourself: he's in great shape... strong as steel," he protested.

An image came into Pam's mind—a nightmare image. And she knew why she understood Gary's fears so well. It had been only a few weeks before that her father had shown up at the Ewing barbeque, sober and standing on his own two feet. By the end of the day he had been reduced to a whimpering, angry drunk, intoxicated to the point of delirium, his hard won progress ruined, as it had been so often before, by Jock Ewing.

"Just a few weeks ago," she reminded her husband, "my daddy came to Southfork for a Ewing barbeque. He was in great shape, too, hadn't had a drink in months..."

Bobby shook his head, interrupting her. "It's different, honey. Digger's not a Ewing—Gary is," he insisted.

Pam's eyes welled up with tears of fury. How could Bobby be so blind? "Digger is my father. He's *my* family. But after Jock Ewing was through with him, he was drunk out of his mind, and his recovery was ruined."

Bobby could see that his wife was upset, and he tried to calm her and at the same time bring the conversation back to Gary. "That's true, but..." he began.

She cut him off. "And he's been a wreck since

that day. He won't even speak to me..." The tears choked her voice. She longed for her father to love her again, to forgive her for marrying the man she loved, who happened to be a Ewing. She longed for him to recover, to regain his dignity, his humanity. Her anger at Jock was great, but even greater was her desire to spare Gary her father's anguish. She grabbed Bobby's two hands in hers and pleaded with him. "Don't put your brother in that same impossible situation. He's too good a person."

Bobby removed his hands from his wife's grasp and stroked her hair. "We won't put him in that position, Pam," he tried to reassure her. "Gary's one of our family. His place is with us. He knows that as well as I do," he added.

It hadn't occurred to Pam, but Bobby was probably right. Family is family, she knew from personal experience, even when everyone is worlds apart, physically and emotionally. Gary probably did miss his home, in spite of his dread of returning. "Do one thing for me," she said, conceding his point, "don't do anything without consulting him first."

It was a small price to pay for his wife's peace of mind. "Whatever you say," Bobby nodded. He kissed his wife tenderly on the lips, and, ending the discussion on a happy, peaceful note, he added, "Now that's enough talking. I'm going outside and burn till I'm the color of charcoal." And with that, he headed for the bedroom to change into his swimsuit. But he was so sure of Gary's intention to return that he couldn't resist adding, over his shoulder, "Mama's going to go nuts. Gary was always her boy, the one she favored most. He was the one with the Southworth in him, she used to say..." He went into the bedroom in the best of spirits.

Pam's face fell. A Southworth among Ewings, Bobby had said. Why did it make her think of a sheep among wolves? A sense of foreboding gripped her again. She was surer than ever that a storm was approaching—a storm that would hit them all, and blow their lives in unknown, dangerous directions.

Chapter Four

On the ride back to Southfork, Jock wondered why everyone was being so quiet. For a while, he'd tried to lighten the atmosphere by telling some stories and a few jokes. Normally, he was considered a man with a fine sense of humor and a fair ability to spin a tale, but not only didn't he get a laugh out of anybody in the car, they'd barely paid attention to him—no more than a grunt here or there to indicate they knew he was speaking! So, after a while, he'd given it up, and sat back quietly and glumly like all the rest of them.

He looked at them one by one, trying to divine the reasons for their stony silences. J.R.'s wasn't hard to figure out. Jock was no fool, and he could tell that if it hadn't been for Sue Ellen, J.R. wouldn't have come at all. He was grateful to his boy for coming anyway, and keeping him company at the auction, especially since he knew J.R. had no taste for it and had no obligation to come along. He remembered himself in the old days. He, too, would have had his patience and good humor worn thin by the smells and noises of the long auction. Things had changed for him now—he felt warm and at home with the animals and the range. He wanted more than anything now to be able to stay out of the turmoil and intrigue of the oil business. How troubled J.R. looked! Always having to worry about things. Jock wouldn't have traded with him for the world.

Ray, however, was a different matter, and Jock was totally puzzled. Ever since he'd come back from the Western store with Lucy, he'd looked troubled and upset. That wasn't like Ray—not at all. And Lucy, while peaceful, was hardly in the same car with them at all. Her mind seemed to be as far away as the stars, and just as misted over. What had gone on at that Western store? Had the two of them had a fight? They always seemed to get along so well. And if they'd had a fight, why was Lucy not upset as well?

Jock shook his head. All this thinking was giving him a headache. Chasing the questions from his mind, he turned his head, and, looking out the window of the car toward the bright red ball of the setting sun, the old man allowed himself to become absorbed in the passing rangeland, its beauty and endless majesty.

Over in the corner of the huge, yet stylish restaurant, the jazz combo played quietly, the throb of the bass vibrating through the room, warming the atmosphere, melding with the clinking of glasses and the clicking of forks and knives. As Pam entered the room, her eyes searched for Gary. In the dim light, it was hard to make out people's faces, but after a moment, Pam saw him, huddled over his club soda at a quiet table far away from both the band and the kitchen door. He was staring down into his drink as if looking for answers at the bottom of his glass. It was clear that he wasn't finding any. Pam made her way over to his table, weaving her way in and around the circular tables, letting the snatches of desultory conversation waft over her like a desert breeze.

She pondered Gary as she approached. How handsome he was, yet how different he looked from Bobby and J.R. In fact, he was the picture of his mother, Ellie. The same kind, blue eyes, the same sandy blonde hair. 'A Southworth among Ewings,' the phrase came back to her, and she shuddered with dread for him.

"Hello, stranger," she said, as she reached his table. Gary looked up and saw her for the first time.

"Greetings," he smiled as he stood up. Then he noticed that Pam was alone. "Where's the big fella?" he asked, as he pulled out her chair.

"He got ambushed by a bunch of carousing oilmen. He won't be long—I hope." Actually, the truth was that while Bobby had stopped to talk to some people in the lobby of the hotel, she had really wanted to talk to Gary alone, to prepare him for Bobby's friendly onslaught.

"Gary..." she began, "Bobby is sure that you want to come back to Southfork with us." She stopped speaking, waiting for his reaction. Gary didn't answer right away. Instead, he sat stock still for a moment, then lifted his glass to his lips— more to wet them than to drink. He swallowed hard, holding the cold glass to his forehead for a second or two, and smiled sheepishly at Pam.

"I can't deny the thought has crossed my mind."

So Bobby had been right after all, at least about that, Pam mused to herself. Still, she knew she was right about Gary's fear, and she felt it was her duty to make him come out with it, so that he could rationally weigh his options. She wanted to help him, to spare him any more pain. "But you haven't decided for certain whether or not to come," she ventured, trying to draw him out further.

Gary took a deep breath, and exhaled. "I'll tell you, Pam...over the last few years I've given it a lot of thought," he told her. "I don't believe I harbor any hard feelings toward J.R. anymore... nor toward my daddy. On the other hand, if I never saw them again it would be all right with me. As far as Mama is concerned, I really do miss her a lot, but I've lived with it till now, and I guess I could go on living with it. But..." His voice trailed off into the mist of sadness. In his eyes was the weariness of a lifetime spent battling tremendous odds.

Pam knew what he was trying to say, and finished his sentence for him. "Lucy?" she asked.

Gary nodded slowly. His daughter had come to mean more to him than anything else in his life. True, he had never known her, but she had become a symbol for him, a symbol of his own weakness and low character for running out on her.

All at once an idea occurred to Pam, a way to solve the problems of avoiding Southfork, yet reuniting Gary and his daughter. "Couldn't we arrange a meeting between you ... someplace else?'' she suggested, knowing that Bobby would be angry with her for bringing up the idea.

Gary looked long and deeply at his sister-in-law. How brave and strong she was, he couldn't help thinking. And, with a smile, he thought how good it was that she had befriended him. He needed her friendship, badly. It might make the difference for him. He thought for a moment about what to do, then leaned forward and began to speak.

"Pam," he said softly, but with the intensity born of suffering, "you were right when you said we have a lot in common. We're both outsiders, you and I."

Pam nodded in agreement. "Me even more than you," she said.

"Yes, that's true," Gary agreed, "and yet you manage to live at Southfork with all of them. I'm sure they don't make it easy for you, yet there you are..."

It was true, she thought. They hadn't made it easy for her, hadn't tried to include her, to accept her. The Barnes name was still anathema around the Ewing household.

"J.R. tries his best, anyway," she conceded, "and Sue Ellen—his wife."

Gary took her hands in his and leaned in to her. "But you survive there," he whispered. "I believe that with your example in front of me, I can make it, Pamela. I'm not one hundred percent sure, but I believe I can. And it would make it a lot easier for me if I could..." He paused for a moment, and looked her straight in the eye. "If I could be sure you'd be there for me to lean on...just in case it's a lot harder for me than I think it's going to be."

His words worried Pam. Her life at Southfork

was hard as it was. Could she help and support someone else as well? Did she have it in her? "But you're asking to use me as a crutch, and if you feel you need a crutch..." she started to say.

Gary cut her off in mid-sentence. His mind was made up. "Listen, if both a man's legs are broken a crutch can be a useful item, don't you think?"

Pam smiled. Perhaps he would be all right, after all. His sense of humor was a strong weapon in his own defense. Maybe she was blowing things out of proportion. After all, Gary was a Ewing—J.R. and Jock wouldn't be as cruel to him as they'd been to Digger—and to her. At least she hoped they wouldn't.

Looking up, Gary saw Bobby entering the restaurant, looking around for them. He stood up and waved, and Bobby, catching sight of him, began to thread his way over to their table. "Sorry—I guess Pam told you I was detained," he said as soon as he arrived.

Without waiting for his brother to sit down, Gary made his announcement. "Bobby, Pam and I have been discussing it...and I think I want to go back to Southfork with you."

Bobby nearly jumped up in the air and cheered out loud. He knew it! He knew Gary would want to come home! Of course he did—Southfork was where he belonged! Reaching across the table, he grasped his brother's hand and held it between both of his. Turning to his wife, he said, surer of himself than ever, "What did I tell you, Pammy? See?" And then, turning back to Gary, he got down to business. "We'll leave about nine tomorrow morning, okay? Mama's going to flip when she hears about this!" He laughed out loud from sheer pleasure. Gary, too, managed a weak smile, the best he could do, considering how difficult the decision had been for him. He glanced at Pam, tentatively, and saw that she, too, had a smile on her face. She wished him the best; she truly did. But her heart told her there were hard times ahead.

It was early in the morning on Southfork Ranch. The coyotes' howls faded into the distance, and the Bantam rooster's call floated over to the house. Soon the orange ball of the sun rose, enormous and sizzling, over the flat Texas horizon, and a new day began—a day that would prove to be an eventful one for Southfork and its residents.

Miss Ellie was the first one up, as usual. Raoul and Teresa were already bustling around downstairs setting up the table for the family's breakfast. After they had all eaten, Sue Ellen and J.R. went out to the garage. They were dressed for the city and were on their way into town. Jock followed them outside. He had a few things he wanted to discuss with J.R. before his son left for town. Jock may have retired from the daily business, but he still kept his hand in. Ewing Oil was still his company, after all, and J.R. would have to listen to his advice whether he agreed with it or not.

Lucy also went outside. Mrs. Ewing, alone of the family members, was still in the house when the phone rang. Raoul came out of the kitchen. "Telephone for you, Mrs. Ewing," he said politely. Ellie followed him into the kitchen, where she picked up the extension. It was early for anyone to be calling. She hoped it wasn't bad news. Ellie always dreaded getting unexpected phone calls.

Ellie couldn't believe what Bobby was telling her. Gary, at last, was coming home. Ellie felt almost faint, and leaned against the kitchen counter to steady herself. She asked Bobby to give her the news once again, to let it sink in properly. Bobby wanted to be sure they were all there for Gary's homecoming. "Yes, Bobby," she replied incredulously, "of course, we'll all be here. All right," she concluded, wanting to get off the phone and give herself time to digest the incredible news. "You remember to buckle up, now. Bye."

After she hung up, her expression remained frozen for a long time. She wasn't aware of the world around her. When she finally came out of it, she saw Raoul looking at her with a quizzical expression on his face. Only then did the recognition of what she had been told begin to sink in. "Did I say 'buckle up?' " Miss Ellie asked, not believing she had said something so mundane in the face of the unbelievable news she'd been handed.

"Yes, Mrs. Ewing," Raoul replied.

"I really said that, didn't I?" Miss Ellie repeated, the news now hitting her with its full impact. "Oh, my goodness," she said out loud to herself, and again, "Oh, my goodness!" Moving toward the door, she cried out, "Jock!" and ran outside to share the great news.

J.R. and Sue Ellen were already seated in *Ewing 3*, and Jock, bending over the open window on the driver's side, was giving J.R. some last minute business instructions. Ellie hurried toward the car, hoping to stop them before J.R. and Sue Ellen drove off. "Jock! Jock!" she cried again.

Now Jock raised himself to his full height and turned to face his wife. Seeing her feverish, frenzied manner, he walked toward her, worried. "What's going on?" he shouted to her. "What's the matter?"

As she reached her husband, Ellie broke out into full-fledged happy laughter, and tears stained her cheeks at the same time. "Nothing. There isn't anything the matter," she rejoiced. "He's on his way home!"

What was she babbling about, Jock wondered. "Huh? Who's on his way?" he demanded to know.

"Gary. Our son is coming home. Today."

As they got out of the car, J.R. and Sue Ellen exchanged worried glances. Happy in Jock's arms, Ellie poured out her good news in a rush. "He bumped into Bobby and Pam at the oilmen's junket. I mean," she corrected herself, "he didn't bump into them; he found them! He's doing well. They're all on their way here right this minute!" And, turning to her eldest son, she cried joyfully, "Did you hear what I said, J.R.? Gary's coming home."

J.R. Ewing smiled the biggest smile he could muster. He had always been expert at feigning emotions, even as a small child he could fake tears or laughter, rage or tenderness, and he had refined his skills over the years. He found that they were of great help to him in life, and now was one of those moments. His smile looked genuine as he said, "I heard you, Mama. I heard every word you said."

Ellie took him by the arm, pleased to see him so glad about Gary's return. "So never mind about going in to work today," she ordered. Turning to her daughter-in-law, she added, "And Sue Ellen, you'll want to stay here, too."

Sue Ellen smiled sweetly. "Of course, Miss Ellie," she said, with a demure little nod.

Ellie felt she ought to apologize for being so domineering. It was rare that she took the reins so boldly—that was the sort of thing she usually left for Jock to take care of. So she began, by way of explaining herself, "Because it's only fitting that he should be welcomed by all of us when he gets here..." She paused, a whiff of uncertainty beginning to invade her consciousness, then continued, "...to give him the kind of homecoming..." She stopped and looked at J.R. Memories began to flood her head—memories of what J.R. and her husband had done all those years ago. She opened her mouth to speak, but no words would come.

J.R. finished her sentence for her. "...the kind of homecoming we Ewings are famous for!" he said robustly.

Ellie stepped over to her son and looked up into his face, searching for the truth behind his heartening words. Was he sincere, or was he lying to her, to all of them? There was no way of knowing with J.R., she knew, and so she warned him, "I don't want anything to spoil this."

"Why, Mama," protested J.R., looking as hurt as an abandoned puppy, "neither do any of us." He looked around at the others for support, as if to say he'd been unjustly accused of some terrible crime. Ellie continued staring up into his eyes.

"Nothing *will* spoil it," she said. It was a parting shot, and after she waited a moment for it to hit its mark, she turned and said to her husband, who had also borne large responsibility for her favorite son's disappearance, "You understand, Jock? Whatever has happened has happened. It's dead and buried. Don't dig it up."

She could not have been clearer. She looked from one of them to the other and back again. "He's still one of us," she said to Jock, imploring his cooperation and warning him to behave at the same time. "You make sure he feels he can fit back in. Don't go putting up obstacles...either of you," she concluded.

Jock's face clouded over, his normally florid complexion darkening with rage. Without a word, he turned and marched back toward the house. Ellie wondered if she'd made a terrible mistake. Had she overstepped her bounds? Was her own husband now turning against her, just when she needed him most? "Jock!" she shouted after him, but he just kept walking. "Jock, did you hear what I said?"

The patriarch of the Ewing clan spun on his heels to face his wife. He was enraged, and he made no effort to spare her his fury. "What kind of monster do you think I am, Ellie?" he bellowed in righteous rage. "I'm not thinking about setting up obstacles. I'm thinking how to get rid of them. I want it to work out just as much as you do." His rage now spent, he admonished his wife, "You ought to know me better than that, Ellie." Hurt to the quick, and still feeling the burden of his son's departure all those years ago, Jock Ewing turned away again and walked slowly, deliberately, back into the house.

Ellie stared after him, admiring the wonderful man she had married, the man who was proud enough to defend his wounded honor, yet humble enough to admit that he had been wrong, very wrong. And, what was most important, the man was willing, with all his heart, to make amends. Silently, she followed her husband inside.

J.R. stood rooted to his spot for a moment or two looking after his mother, then turned to face his wife. He was surprised to see she'd been studying him, watching his reactions. That was just like Sue Ellen, he thought with disdain, always trying to get inside my head. Smirking with disapproval, he went back to the car to collect his briefcase, then slammed the door as hard as he could and headed for the house.

As he passed his wife, she stopped him with her arm. "Isn't this a wonderful surprise?" she said sarcastically. J.R. just glowered at her, saying nothing. "For Lucy, above all," she added. Jealousy gleamed green in her eyes.

"Good for Lucy," agreed J.R. breaking away from her and continuing toward the house.

Staring after him, Sue Ellen realized that something would have to be done, even if she had to do it herself.

Chapter Five

Southfork Ranch was big in the way things can be big only in the state of Texas. It covered two hundred thousand-odd acres of flat rangeland, and had several creeks and lakes interspersed throughout the property. There were stands of trees, mostly along the banks of the creeks and lakes, but in general, the vegetation consisted of scrub and meadow grass. It was typical of the spreads that used to exist all over the state. However, many of those spreads had given way to oil derricks, urban sprawl, condo parks and shopping malls, as people flooded the sunbelt in search of the good life. In a sense, Southfork was the last of the great ranches—an oasis in an ever-expanding land of humanity and industry.

As noon approached, Lucy sat in the brush at the side of one of the larger and more secluded lakes, a picnic basket of fruit prepared by Teresa at her side. As she peeled an orange, she gazed at the ducks and geese swimming lazily on the shimmering surface of the water, as placid as the day itself. Jimmy Monahan lay next to her, watching her intently out of the corner of his eye, trying, as he always did, to get some sort of a fix on her feelings toward him. She had rarely shown him much favor, just enough to keep him on the string. Jimmy was intelligent enough to know he was being used, but he was also enough in love to forgive Lucy's behavior and to hope it would change in his favor. Lately, however, her behavior seemed to be veering in the opposite direction. She had become more and more distant toward him, barely concealing her impatience with his demands for attention. He knew they were headed for a showdown, and soon.

Lucy threw away the orange peel and turned to Jimmy, a worried expression in her eyes. "Are you going to be working the night shift for a long time, do you think?" she asked.

Jimmy hesitated, wondering what she meant. "Till the boss puts me back on the day shift," he replied. "Why do you ask?"

Lucy shrugged, as if it were a matter of indifference to her. "'Cause I'll be starting school again soon. With you working nights, how're we going to get together?"

Jimmy raised his eyebrows. Here was a shred of hope at last. He had to know how she felt about him, and he had to know now. Disguising his feelings with an air of playfulness, he ventured, "Do you care whether we do or not?"

Lucy, tough as nails, shot right back, "Of course I care. How else am I going to get to see my mama?"

No matter how long Jimmy knew her, Lucy's

bluntness always came as a shock to him. But this time he wasn't going to let her off the hook until he had an answer. He was tired of having his nose rubbed in the mud by the girl he loved. "Other than that," he pressed her.

The contrary streak in Lucy that always came to the surface when she was challenged in any way answered for her now. "Not really. Well, maybe just a little."

Jimmy smiled. As nasty as she was being, she was still holding out a little hope to him. "That's by far the nicest thing you've ever said to me," he blurted out, in his confusion of hurt and hope.

It was the wrong thing to say. All Lucy's spitefulness rose to the fore. She'd be damned if she'd let anyone have a claim on her affections, especially Jimmy Monahan. "In that case, I didn't mean a word of it," she said, cruelly.

Jimmy felt something inside him snap. He hurled the fruit he was eating as far as he could into the lake, scattering the birds into the air and shattering the peace of the tranquil lakeside scene. "Well, I care whether or not we get together," he said, his voice rising in spite of himself.

"That's not my problem," Lucy shot right back, half playfully, half truthfully.

Jimmy felt he had overstepped his bounds, and in an effort to save the situation, he said, "Quit it, Lucy. I'm trying to carry on a serious discussion with you."

"You're trying too hard," quipped Lucy, not giving an inch.

"I think you're the greatest," Jimmy pleaded, desperate to get back in her good graces.

"Then you must not be thinking clearly," she

replied, packing what was left of the fruit in the basket.

It was true. Lucy had very little regard for herself. And as a result, anyone who thought as much of her as Jimmy Monahan obviously did wasn't worth much to her either. She got up and started back in the direction of the house. Jimmy, alarmed, grabbed the basket and scrambled after her. "What's the matter?" he asked, hoping he hadn't blown it with her completely.

"Not a thing," Lucy lied, "I just have to be getting back."

"But—" Jimmy tried in vain to stop her. Lucy brushed past him, and as he stood there looking after her, she ran at full tilt until she was out of sight.

The living room of the mansion at Southfork was decorated traditionally. Miss Ellie had collaborated closely with the interior decorators each time the room had been redone, and she had largely managed to resist changes of style the decorators had wanted to introduce. Sue Ellen often imagined to herself how she would redecorate the room when she came into ownership of Southfork. Ever since she and J.R. had gotten married, she had more or less assumed that one day Southfork would be hers. For more than a few years, she had been the only daughter-in-law, and she was, after all, married to the first-born son, the natural heir, both by birth and by ability. Normally, she harbored no doubts about either her husband's intention or his capacity to keep his parents' inheritance largely for himself. He had the intelligence, the ruthlessness, and a willing helpmeet in her. Everything to insure a smooth and uneventful succession.

Indeed, Jock had turned over the company to J.R. But when Bobby brought home his new wife, things had taken an unforeseen turn. Jock had brought Bobby into the business and was clearly favoring him more and more. Then had come Pam's pregnancy, which glowed all the brighter compared with her own seven-year-long failure. Fortunately, Pam had had a miscarriage, so Sue Ellen's position was safe for the moment. Until today, that is. With Gary on his way back to Southfork, there was no telling what might happen. All her sensors went on alert, ready to pick up any immediate threat.

What disturbed Sue Ellen was her husband's unexpected attitude. He had been so nonchalant, even happy, about his brother's unforeseen return. Whatever he was feeling, he hadn't seen fit to share those feelings with her. And there he was now, casually hanging a painting on the living room wall. In contrast to all the other paintings at Southfork, which, if not all masterpieces, were at least professionally done, this one was a mere sketch, and by an amateur, too, if a gifted one. It was a loosely drawn pair of wild stallions, obviously unfinished, though it was mounted on an expensive, elaborate oak frame. J.R. struggled to mount the heavy frame on its hooks. Sue Ellen smirked, guessing correctly what was going on. "That must be one of Gary's masterpieces," she said, more than a hint of sarcasm in her voice.

J.R. did not look down. He was trying to level the painting, not an easy task, and in any case, he didn't have to look at his wife to catch the tone of her remark. He chose to ignore it for the moment. "The best one I could lay my hands on," he said, tonelessly. "Mama wanted to have something of his hanging up." Now the painting was level, and J.R. stepped away to check it.

Sue Ellen took a quick look around. There was nobody in sight or in earshot. Now was as good a time as any to get down to brass tacks. "What do you suppose made him want to come home?" she asked, broaching the subject.

"How do I know?" replied J.R., crossing over to the liquor cabinet and pouring himself a shot of bourbon. "To see his daughter, maybe."

Sue Ellen could see now that there was more going on inside her husband than met the eye. This visit had surely upset him. "J.R.," she admonished him, "it's not even noon." Ignoring her, J.R. downed the drink in one fast gulp. He exhaled, the fire of the whiskey pouring down his gullet. The warmth of it steadied him, and leaning back against the table, he stared across the room at the painting he had just mounted on the wall.

Sue Ellen resumed her probing. "There must be something he wants," she said.

J.R. could see he wasn't going to get away without some sort of explanation. Reassuringly, he said, "He's too dumb to want anything. And even if he did, he's not strong enough to go after it."

Sue Ellen found it hard to imagine a Ewing who was anything other than strong. "Maybe he's different than he was."

J.R. snorted. "I hardly think so," he murmured, remembering his brother as a child. "He was always weak." The memories flooded back to him. He had genuinely liked his brother, and at one time they had been quite close.

"That why you got rid of him?" she asked, digging for an answer.

J.R. wheeled on her menacingly. The look in his eyes was lethal. She shrank back as he spat out, "I never tried to get rid of him. He's my brother. I tried to save his future. We had his life all planned out for him; he'd just started going to the university. We did everything we could to help him correct that terrible mistake he'd made, marrying that piece of trash..."

It was all true, J.R. reflected. He had nearly killed that girl. She had ruined the family's peace and happiness, and things had never been the same since.

Sue Ellen had the explanation she wanted. She understood now that J.R.'s family loyalty was driving him to betray his best self-protective instincts. In an effort to draw him out further, she prodded, "Only you wound up getting rid of him instead of the girl..."

J.R. was lost in the memories. That girl...he'd like to have wrung her neck. "He ran off and she was stuck here," he remembered. "He left without a trace...I don't know what he was so frightened of. That's the way he always was, running away from every little thing. Even as little kids...I always had to fight all his battles for him, I remember. I made sure nobody beat him up—they knew they'd have to deal with me after." His voice faltered. He remembered how his brother had worshipped him. It was the closest he'd ever felt to being a father. Now Gary was coming back, but their relationship would never be the same.

It was all clear to Sue Ellen now. But she had to know where her husband stood. Could she rely on him, she wondered. She had to know. Her future was at stake. "Suppose he wants to stay on here," she postulated. "Look how much trouble Bobby's caused you since he's come into the business. How're you going to handle two brothers?"

It was a direct challenge, but J.R. refused to answer it. "He's coming for a visit, Sue Ellen," he insisted. "I'm happy about that because he's my brother."

"But what happens if—" Sue Ellen pressed.

J.R. interrupted her, overriding her insistence with his own powerful certainty. "He won't be staying around for long," he said firmly. "He's a born loser, and he'll always be a loser. Every time he wants something, he loses it, screws it up. It won't be any different this time. Even if he does want something, he'll screw it up and be gone. I won't even have to lift a finger. Believe me, darlin'."

Having said his piece, and firmly convinced he was right, J.R. rose to leave. As he passed the picture, he stopped to straighten it. Suddenly the weight of the oak frame dislodged the hooks and sent it crashing to the ground. The glass covering the drawing shattered all over the floor. J.R. turned to Sue Ellen, and smiling his brightest smile said, "What did I tell you?" He laughed quietly and without picking up the fallen artwork, he walked out of the room in the best of moods.

As they drove home from the airport, *Ewing 4*'s wheels rolling smoothly down expressways which hadn't existed the last time he had been in Dallas,

Gary stared out the rear window, silently taking it all in. The new skyscrapers, the massive traffic, even at noon, all the people...a lot can happen in sixteen years, he thought to himself—a whole lot. Riding through the heart of town, Gary found it hard to believe he'd been away so long and had never once visited. It hit him now how great his fear was of returning to his native city, to his home, to his family. He wondered once again if he was up to it. Oh, well, he thought, smiling wistfully, it was too late to turn back now, even if he wanted to. Already they were in Braddock, approaching the vicinity of Southfork. One by one, he pictured the members of his family and how he imagined they reacted to the news of his coming. What did they all think of him, he wondered. And how would they act when they actually saw him?

Bobby glanced at his brother in the rear-view mirror but did not intrude upon his reveries. He knew deep inside that Gary needed time to reflect, to get his bearings, before he confronted the family head on. His right hand reached out for Pamela's and gripped it hard. He felt her answering pressure. She understood. She always did. Bobby thought to himself once again, as he often did, what a wonderful woman he had married.

If Bobby had turned his eyes from the road to look at his wife, he would have seen how troubled she was. To her it was like reliving her own arrival at Southfork, and the pain of that memory filled her heart as they approached the ranch. Poor Gary, she thought. She hoped the pressure wouldn't be too much for him, but something told her it would.

***

Instead of heading directly back to the house from the lake, Lucy took a detour down a dirt road in the direction of the stables. She hoped Ray Krebbs would be there. Seeing his jeep parked outside, she searched for him in the stables. When she couldn't find him, she assumed he must be in the hayloft.

"Ray? You up in the loft, or what?"

She heard his footsteps on the ceiling. "I'll be right down," she heard him say in a muffled voice. But instead of waiting for him to come down to her, she climbed up, surprising Ray, who was just about to start down.

"Didn't I say I'd be right down?" asked Ray, not a little miffed. Her treatment of him the day before had upset him quite a bit, and he still wasn't over it.

"I thought I'd come up!" Lucy said cheerfully.

Apparently, thought Ray, she's not going to tell the family after all. Still, he wondered why she was being so nice.

Lucy looked around the hayloft. "I'm sorry about the way I treated you yesterday, Ray," she said softly, "it was a terrible thing to do to a friend, but I had no choice."

Something was fishy about all this niceness, Ray thought. "Why the sudden turnaround?" he asked.

Lucy shrugged. "Oh, Jimmy and I had a fight. I'm not sure I'll be seeing him anymore."

"What's that got to do with me?" said Ray, puzzled.

"We're old friends, Ray. I can tell you the truth. I wasn't really going out with Jimmy—he was just driving me someplace. Someplace I couldn't get to any other way. Now that he and I are, well, on the outs, I guess you could say, I've got no way to get there. And so I thought, being old friends and all..."

"That I'd step in as your chauffeur?" Ray finished her sentence for her. So that was what it had all been about! Well, at least whoever it was she was seeing, it wasn't a Barnes. Nevertheless, he wasn't about to get involved in any of Lucy's romantic adventures. That way lay only trouble. He was about to turn her down flat when he saw that she was glancing intently out the window.

Stepping to her side, Ray followed her look. In the distance, *Ewing 4* had pulled into the driveway, and Bobby and Pam were getting out. They weren't due back until the next day, Ray remembered. So did Lucy, apparently, for she asked, without turning her glance away, "How come Bobby and Pam came home so early?" It was highly unusual for the Ewings to change their schedules, particularly when a function like the oilmen's junket was involved.

To get a closer look, Ray took down the binoculars. Looking at the scene in front of the house, he could see what Lucy must have seen from the very beginning — somebody else was getting out of the car with Bobby and Pam; a tall, blonde-haired man, whose face looke somewhat familiar to Ray.

Now he could see Miss Ellie, dressed in her finest daytime dress, running over to the newcomer and throwing her arms around his neck. The two embraced tightly for a long time. "Could it be..." thought Ray. It was beginning to dawn on him who the stranger must be.

"Who's that man, Ray?" Lucy asked impatiently, and without waiting for an answer from Ray, snatched the binoculars away from him. Although he binoculars afforded her a much closer perspective of the touching scene in front of the house, the stranger's face was turned in the opposite direction, and she could only see his back.

"Do you know him?" she asked again, already feeling inside herself who it was, who it had to be. Now she could see Jock emerging from the house and, approaching the new arrival, shaking his hand slowly, almost shyly. The blood began to course through her temples, pounding through her brain, as the knowledge penetrated the veils of her mind, slowly seeping into her consciousness. Lucy lowered the binoculars and wetting her dry lips, she turned to Ray.

"Ray, is that..." But the words wouldn't come, not for either of them. Ray simply stared at her, an earnest, almost shaken expression on his face.

The incredible truth dawned on Lucy now in its full force. She shot to her feet, and without another word, crossed the hayloft and disappeared in a flash down the ladder, the binoculars still in her hand.

Ray turned back toward the window. Now he could see Lucy running across the wide lawn that separated the stables from the manor house. The man, whose identity Ray now knew for certain, detached himself from his mother and turned toward the approaching figure, knowing at once who she was. He stepped a few feet away from his parents, so as to make his meeting with his daughter a more private one.

Ray felt the privacy of the moment keenly, and he turned away for a moment. Thoughts of his own father rushed into his head. Amos Krebbs, that no-good scoundrel, who had left his wife with her small son, unable to take care of him. For Ray, there would never be a reunion like this one, and the sadness and pain of the knowledge rushed through him like an express train. Feeling it would be less painful to witness the scene below than to give in to his own tragic thoughts, Ray turned his eyes once again to the window.

Lucy had stopped running and stood several feet from her father on the lawn. The two of them faced each other, both eager yet afraid to close the distance between them, to hold each other close for the first time. Finally, Gary broke the silence.

"Hello, baby," he said, his voice choked with emotion.

"Hi, Daddy," replied Lucy, on the verge of both laughter and tears.

"You're a sight for sore eyes," said her father, feeling keenly the inadequacy of words to such a moment.

"So are you, Daddy," said his daughter.

Perhaps it was the word 'Daddy' that finally broke the moment, for now Gary extended his hand to Lucy, smiling as he did so. His daughter, his full-grown baby girl, was a vision of heaven right before his eyes. His heart was full to bursting, and tears trickled out of his eyes.

Lucy reached out and took her father's hand, feeling for the first time in her life like a complete, whole person, feeling that she would never let go of him again. Holding each other's hands so tightly that it hurt, the two of them turned toward the house, walking silently together side by side, the weight of sixteen years apart pressing on both their hearts, the miracle of their reunion making them feel lighter than air. Ellie and Jock fell into step behind them, also holding hands, and behind them, Bobby and Pam, their arms around each other.

From his perch in the hayloft, Ray watched them go until they were all inside the house. He ran his fist across his face, wiping the tears from his cheeks. He had never felt so alone—so finally, hopelessly alone.

Chapter Six

The night was cool and dry. Outside the crickets chirped by the thousands in the utter blackness, and in the depths of the dark surrounding the ranch, coyotes howled to each other. A chill was in the air, and the wind blew the dust in all directions. But inside the mansion, the warm glow of the fire emanated into the whole room, reflecting in its reds and oranges the reunited Ewing clan.

The family sat quietly gazing into the fire, watching the flames play on each other. On the sofa sat Gary and Lucy, close to each other, holding hands as they had done almost continuously since their reunion on the lawn that afternoon. Lucy's face was relaxed in utter peace and happiness. Her eyes glittered with the flames' reflection, and with the tears that kept coming. Her nostrils flared as she breathed in contentment, and her smile was angelic. She could almost have been mistaken for a little girl, sweet as only young children can be. With her wholesome looks and her diminutive size, Lucy had often played the schoolgirl; but tonight it was not an act. For once in her life, there was not a wisecrack in her head, or an ungenerous thought.

Her father felt far from peaceful, however. He shared his daughter's joy, but his soul was crammed with other, still unresolved questions. He felt his guts wound up in knots. He had hardly touched his dinner. Miss Ellie had felt hurt a bit, though she would never have let it show. He'd always loved her cooking as a child. But in the enormity of her joy, she'd ignored the telling signs of his uneasy and troubled state. Sitting on Gary's other side, she wore almost the exact same expression as her granddaughter: perfect peace and contentment. Amazing, thought Gary, that they're both so unaware of what's going on inside me. Can I be that good a liar, he wondered?

The rest of the family was spread out on chairs around the fire. They seemed to share, to one degree or another, Gary's discomfort, but no one was more fidgety than Jock. He shifted around in his chair continually, his eyes roving to all the far corners of the room—anywhere but on his son's face.

All evening they'd managed to avoid the burning question of Gary's departure. But in avoiding it, they'd been forced to make nothing but small talk. It was the sense of things unspoken that was making Gary so uncomfortable, and that feeling was mounting with each passing tick of the Grandfather clock in the corner. He almost wished they were screaming at each other at the top of their lungs. It would make him feel more at

ease, more at home. He had run out of small talk
long ago, but since nobody else seemed able to say
anything at all, Gary felt compelled to say
something.

"It's hard to believe how much the same the
place looks," he blurted out. He sounded stupid to
himself, and wished he'd been able to keep his
mouth shut.

To Miss Ellie, the conversation could not have
been more natural. She understood that things
would take time to heal, and that they had to be
treated gently and delicately if they weren't to be
aggravated. "Oh, there are quite a few changes,"
she laughed. "This living room set..."

"But it all has the same *feeling*," Gary corrected
her. It was true—the same heavy feeling of
oppression gripped him now as it had before he'd
left.

"It must be something about the architecture
that makes it feel that way," said Jock, with a
helpless tone in his voice.

Miss Ellie laughed, but it didn't lighten the
atmosphere in the room. "Gary wasn't talking
about the architecture, Jock, at least, I don't think
so," she said needlessly.

Jock was well aware of what Gary had meant;
more keenly aware, in fact, than Miss Ellie. He
scowled at her, displeased that she had corrected
him in front of the whole family. Jock hated being
embarrassed.

Gary noticed Jock's expression and felt he had
to deflect his father's annoyance. "I don't know
what I was talking about," he lied. "Maybe the
humidity or something." What an asinine
remark, he thought to himself. And to change the

subject completely, he turned to Sue Ellen, whom he'd met for the first time that afternoon and said, "Sue Ellen, I understand from Lucy that you're the finest rider in the state these days."

Actually, Lucy had told him a lot more than that, most of it extremely unfavorable, but he wanted to give Sue Ellen the chance to make her own impression on him, and besides, Gary was trying to make friends. It was his best chance of laying those old ghosts to rest.

Sue Ellen had been aloof to him so far, but his remark brought a genuine smile to her face. She blushed slightly and replied with false modesty, "That's very nice of her, but she's exaggerating a bit."

"It's not an exaggeration at all," said Pam, not a little annoyed at Sue Ellen's southern belle act.

Jock Ewing had had about all he could stand. "I got a suggestion," he boomed. "Why don't we quit talkin' about doilies and get down to what's really going on!"

The atmosphere in the room turned tense. They all knew he was right, but none of them was anxious to have a confrontation, then or ever.

"Jock! Hush!" Miss Ellie cried in alarm. But it was too late to stop him now that he'd broken the ice.

"It was hard enough to take all through dinner," he snapped, overriding her objection, "but I can't stand it any longer!"

Bobby saw his mother's alarm, and the family conciliator in him came to the fore.

"Daddy," he said gently with a protective glance at his mother, "I think there's a lot to be discussed—too much to cover in one sitting."

Whatever fine qualities Jock Ewing may have had, sensitivity to other people's feelings was not one of them. What was good for him was bound to be good for everybody else, he felt, and to be fair, if one judged by past history, he was usually right.

"No, there isn't!" he insisted, slapping his hand on his knee for emphasis. "Not if we keep it simple. Who hurt who? Who needs to be forgiven, and who needs to give forgiveness? We can stand up like men and not pull any punches. Anybody want to deck me? I'm ready—step right up and fire away."

Miss Ellie was shocked. She had never imagined he would go so far. The fear of losing her boy once again welled up in her. "You've said enough, Jock," she shouted.

Her outburst silenced Jock. But in the silence that followed, J.R. seized the moment and took center stage. With a big smile on his face, he stood up and crossed to the very center of the room. Right in front of a surprised Gary, he said, "Well, why is what Daddy's saying such a bad idea? I think it's good common sense—in principle, anyway. And I," he continued, pausing a moment for dramatic effect, "am going to be the first to say my piece."

Gary squirmed in anxiety. He, too, wanted more than anything to avoid a fight with his brother. "J.R..." he began, tentatively, but J.R. waved him off.

"No, I've got to get this off my chest," he went on. "Gary, I'd like to say that I feel glad you came back home. It was generous on your part, and I look at it as an opportunity to let bygones be bygones."

There wasn't a sound to be heard in the large living room. No one had been prepared for J.R.'s conciliatory stance. Everyone had been expecting trouble, and he had taken them completely unawares.

After a moment of complete shock, Gary collected himself enough to stammer, "It's all right, J.R. I mean it. It is."

J.R. turned around to the rest of the family, triumphant. "How 'bout that? Gary was always the one with the biggest heart of all of us!" Turning back to Gary on the couch, he said, in a voice only a little too loud and high, "Hey, brother, welcome back. It's good to have you home!"

It was late in the evening now, and most of the family had headed for their bedrooms. J.R.'s magnanimous gesture had gone a long way toward easing their tension, and they went to bed with hearts considerably lightened. On the veranda, Gary and his new-found daughter sat, still hand in hand, talking quietly. It was impossible for Gary to make her understand why he had left her. Yet he did try to convey to her some of his heartbreak to give her a sense of the enormous troubles he'd been through in the intervening years.

For her part, Lucy listened with a forgiving heart. It didn't matter to her anymore why he had gone away; the important thing to her was that she had her father back, and she would never let him go again. She accepted his explanations of why he had left her as a vow never to leave her again. In the peace that knowledge gave her, she drank in her father's words, trying to absorb his whole being, his whole past, in just one evening's conversation.

Finally, with one last hug, they parted for the night, and Lucy went up to her room, leaving her father on the veranda to take one last look at the canopy of stars, one last drink of the black Texas night, before turning in.

Gary strolled a little way out into the darkness, far enough to look back at the house and see it all in a glance. The house had a forbidding size in the darkness of the night, but it also had a reassuring stability, as if nothing could ever budge it from its foundations. Gary smiled at the feeling it gave him, of permanence, of anchor, of reliability.

Suddenly he felt that someone was watching him. Looking up and to the side of the house, he saw a figure on one of the balconies looking down at him intently, hands gripped tightly on the railing. It was J.R.

How long had he been there, watching, listening? A chill went through Gary's body as he stared back at his brother. The light was behind J.R., silhouetting him; still, Gary could make out J.R.'s eyes, as if they were live, glowing coals, the frightening intensity of them, burning into his body, penetrating his very soul. He felt afraid of his brother at that moment, just as he used to. In spite of his brother's soothing words and apparent friendliness, he could not keep the dread from sneaking into his heart. Unable to keep the eye contact any longer, Gary looked away. He walked into the house, feeling J.R.'s glance burning through the back of his head every step of the way, as if his brother were a sharpshooter, lining him up in the sights of his telescopic rifle, measuring him for the kill. For a moment he was terrified.

***

Lying in his bed, the same bed he had slept in as a boy, Gary stared sleeplessly at the ceiling. His life seemed irrevocably split into two different halves, and he found it impossible to put the two halves together. How different the two sides of him were, how unbridgeable the gap seemed to him. He pulled the covers tightly over his body, up to his chin, as if to protect himself from some childhood fear newly risen to haunt him again. He had known he would have trouble sleeping, but he never thought he'd be this wide awake after so tiring and eventful a day.

He tried everything to fall asleep—counting the squares in the wallpaper from floor to ceiling, following the lights behind his eyes when he closed them tightly, even counting sheep—nothing worked, and Gary knew nothing would. Now his stomach began to rumble, as if to remind him that he'd eaten virtually no dinner that night. But Gary wasn't hungry, he was still too upset to eat anything substantial. Perhaps a glass of milk would calm his stomach. He grabbed a bathrobe and made his way down the hallway.

Soundlessly, he crept past J.R.'s door. Though he knew J.R. must be asleep by now, he wondered. In his overtired state, he imagined J.R. crouching behind the door, waiting for him to pass so that he could open the door and pounce on him from behind. Gary shook himself, feeling foolish for allowing such a childish fear to get the better of him, and continued down the stairs, heading for the kitchen.

It was dark, but even after all these years, Gary knew his way around. He could have made his way to the refrigerator with his eyes closed.

As the bright light of the refrigerator came on, he realized that someone was sitting at the kitchen table. He gasped in surprise. So J.R. had been waiting for him after all! But, upon closer scrutiny, he saw that it was not J.R. at all, but his mother.

Gary reached for the lightswitch. "Mama, it's you!" he said, answering her smile with his own relieved one.

"Hello, son," said Miss Ellie softly. "I've been expecting you."

"What made you think I'd be coming down?" he asked, puzzled.

"This," said Miss Ellie, taking the container of milk from his hand and pouring him a glass. As she did so, she continued, "I was sure you'd be coming to the kitchen for your milk. You always did that whenever you couldn't get to sleep at night."

Of course; so that was it! He'd forgotten, but she was right. Unconsciously, he had followed his old childhood pattern. "You knew I'd be lying there awake tonight, didn't you, Mama?" he laughed. How he loved her! She knew him so well, so deeply, and loved him so much. He felt a pang of guilt at having left her and never having written or called all these years.

Ellie shrugged. "You've had a big day..." she explained.

"That's for sure," he nodded in agreement. Smiling, he took a long drink of milk, and felt it going down like some ancient tonic, soothing him, relaxing him.

Ellie stared at him tenderly. "I'll never forget,"

she said, "when Bobby first came home with me from the hospital...you were down for your milk every single night."

Gary was startled by his mother's words. He had no memory of those times, though he'd been old enough to remember—four years old, to be exact. "Was I?" he said, "Why was I so upset?"

Ellie shook her head, bowing before the mystery of life, and the impenetrability of children's hearts. "I guess you were ambivalent," she offered.

"About Bobby?" Gary asked, prodding her on to tell the story.

"About your feelings," she answered. "You were confused, torn. On the one hand, you were crazy about your new brother, and on the other hand, you were frightened ...frightened, I suppose, that you were being replaced as my baby." Ellie's eyes misted over at the memory. Those days had been the most wonderful of her life, and she would remember every last detail of them as long as she lived.

Gary shook his head in admiration and wonder at his mother's recollection. "I have no recollection of that at all." Again the feeling came over him of the huge chasm between his past and his present. He wanted more than anything to build a bridge to that past, to reunite the sundered halves of his existence, and make himself whole again.

Ellie savored the memory. "It happened, all right," she nodded. "Anyhow, I woke up one night, in the middle of the night, and I heard you going for your milk..." She began chuckling. Gary leaned into her, eager to hear what was so funny. "...and there was more noise than I was used to hearing...so I came down to see what was going on." She stopped, overwhelmed with tenderness for him.

"What was I doing?" asked Gary.

"You had heard Bobby whimpering in his crib before we did and you'd decided to take care of the baby the way I sometimes did when he cried. In addition to your milk, you had taken a bottle of formula from the refrigerator and a pot from the cabinet, and you were standing on a chair trying to put the bottle in the pot on the stove... I was so proud of you. This was the way my son Gary dealt with his ambivalence—by sharing his private ritual with the baby brother he found so threatening."

Gary felt overwhelmed by love for his mother. She understood him so well, always had, much better than he understood himself. How ironic that, as much as she loved him, she was so totally unable to help him get over his fears. "You don't really believe I had it all figured out like that?" he asked, doubting that he'd ever had such a generous impulse in him.

"Somewhere deep inside yourself you did," she replied, with unshakable certainty.

If she was so sure of his goodness, what right did he have to doubt himself? He finished the milk, rinsed out the glass, and put it in the dishrack. When he turned around to face her, he saw that she had come up beside him.

"Gary...I've longed for you...every minute of every day," she said, her heart overflowing. He held her tightly in his arms. If only he could undo the hurt he had done her!

"I'm glad I came home, Mama." At that moment,

he felt completely at home with his decision. But even as he held her, the moment passed.

"I'm never going to let you leave again, Gary," said his mother, smiling blissfully. "It's a miracle, you coming back to us, and I'll never stop being thankful for it as long as I live."

The words sank into Gary's consciousness, stirring up a maelstrom of anxiety, undoing all the good the milk and their conversation had done. The black cloud of his fear enveloped him once more, and he felt his destiny moving out of his own hands.

The sun had not yet risen, but the sky was beginning to lighten, the miraculous greens, purples and oranges of dawn painting the horizon in succession, a painting in motion, breathtaking in the distance. The insect sounds of night had quieted down now, replaced by the bird-chirping of early morning and the crowing of the roosters. It was a feathered chorus, a concert virtually unattended by any human audience. There was, however, at least one person up and about that Southfork morning, and his footsteps were a quiet undercurrent to the glorious singing in the trees and tall grasses.

Gary Ewing felt, as he walked the ranch—his ranch—that the chorus of the birds was a welcome especially for him, and that the ranch had opened its earthen arms to take him in again. For the first time since his return the day before, he felt completely whole, totally at peace. Coming upon a pair of steer grazing in the meadow, he leaned against the fence and stroked their warm, soft hides. He knew this was where he belonged. The land was in his soul, and he was a part of it. He loved these steer as if they were his family. And as they shared the dawn together, he felt that they, and all other living things, truly were his family, all part of the same cosmos, sharing the same space and time, with much more uniting them than separating them. His heart was full and he was thankful for the gift of life he had been given. How could he have thrown so much of it away? Whatever happened, he swore to himself, he would keep that awareness and make the most of his moments from now on.

He passed on to the stables, looking for familiar faces among the horses, but too much time had passed. The colts he had known and ridden as a boy were old now, or gone forever, and the horses he saw now in the stalls were their foals, and the foals of their foals. Would he get to know these horses the way he had known their fathers and mothers?

Full of feeling, and with the sun of a new day at his back, Gary walked slowly back toward the house to meet the challenge his family posed for him. The house loomed, its white wood walls gleaming pink in the newly risen sun. So much had happened to him in that house, so many memories. Could he really ever live there again?

As he drew nearer, he saw the door of the house open and Lucy emerge. Waving to him, she came running, her arms open wide. "Hi!" he shouted and, as she approached him, "What are you doing up at this hour?"

Lucy laughed. "I was up all night—too excited to sleep."

He kissed his daughter's hair, put his arm around her, and started to lead her back toward the house. How had he managed to stay away from her so long? He reproached himself bitterly for his cowardice and hugged her tightly as they walked. He would not let her go so easily again.

Now, Lucy detached herself from his grasp and, tugging at his hand, tried to lead him back toward the stables.

"What are you doing, honey?" he asked.

"Sshhhhh," she cautioned him and added, in a whisper, "Quiet. I don't want them to wake up and see us go."

She had an air of conspiracy about her. Gary laughed quietly, playing along with his daughter. "Where are we going?" he whispered back, raising his eyebrows.

"We're taking a little drive to Fort Worth," she answered, pulling him relentlessly away from the house toward the stables.

Gary protested. "Wait a minute; that's a long way to go. . .shouldn't we—"

She cut him off insistently. "I don't want anyone to know where we've gone. Besides, they'll all be asleep for quite a while yet. Please, Daddy," she pleaded, "don't argue with me—the trip will be worth your while, I promise. We'll get the truck from Ray Krebbs, okay? He won't tell, don't worry."

In spite of himself, Gary had to laugh again. His daughter had planned it all out like a general, though for the life of him he didn't know what she could possibly have cooked up for them. Fort Worth, of all places! Shaking his head in admiration, he followed her, submitting to her will. Forgetting his worries about the family, he put himself in her charge.

The diner was busy as the early morning breakfast trade poured in. Truckers, factory workers—all the early risers, too tired, too rushed to cook their own breakfasts, sat themselves down for down for Pete's bacon and eggs special, for the French toast or pancakes and, more than anything else, for the hot, strong coffee they counted on to wake them up and start their long, hard day.

Pete stood by the grill, spatula in his hand, shoveling the food to the plates stacked by his side with one hand, cracking eggs with the other, turning them over just right, and replacing toast in the toaster as fast as it kept popping out. Val, with the sure, steady grace she had acquired during years of waitressing, threaded the small aisle up and down the diner, depositing and picking up the plates, cups and saucers, holding the pot of hot coffee high over her head to keep it from being jostled. The low, steady hum of sleepy morning conversation, punctuated now and then by a raucous laugh, filled the small room. The aroma of bacon was mixed with that of cigarettes, the smoke mingling in the air and wafting through the room.

As the pickup pulled into the parking lot, Gary turned to his daughter in surprise. "Sure you prefer this to your grandma's breakfast?" he asked.

"They've got a special dish here I know you're gonna flip for," she answered coyly. Cutting the motor, she hopped out of the truck, beckoning him to follow.

They opened the screen door and jostled their way in past the customers paying their checks at the cash register. Gary followed Lucy up to the counter where two seats in the center had just become available.

Lucy stood on tiptoe and looked around. Gary wondered what she was searching for. It suddenly became clear to him why they had come here and what Lucy's surprise 'dish' was when he saw her wave to someone.

As Valene approached them, her arms full of dirty dishes, the waving hand caught her eye. She saw her daughter and was slightly taken aback. She hadn't expected her back so soon. It was usually at least a week between their meetings. Val approached, but now her gaze was arrested by the man standing next to her daughter. Lucy had her arms around him, but it wasn't Jimmy Monahan, it was... it was...

The crash of the dishes brought all other noises in the diner to a halt. All eyes turned to the distraught waitress, her chest heaving in alarm, her arms out in front of her, unaware that she had dropped anything at all.

Lucy, too, seemed oblivious to the catastrophe of the broken dishes. She smiled from ear to ear, holding her father's hand in the air for her mother to see.

"Look who I brought, Mama!" she cried, her eyes brimful with happy tears, "It's him! Handsome as ever!"

Chapter Seven

It was still early morning. Bobby and Pam were sleeping soundly, their bodies resting together like spoons, exhausted from the trip to Las Vegas and a night of furious lovemaking. The sheets gently rose and fell with their every peaceful breath, and the light of the morning just barely filtered through the heavy curtains, leaving the room enveloped in darkness. The sound of the telephone ringing downstairs did not even make its way to their door. They slept on, unaware of the crisis that was already in progress.

The knock at the door was so light that at first neither of them stirred. Raoul tried again, but again there was no response. He cleared his throat and said, loudly enough to be heard, "Telephone for Miss Pamela."

Pam opened her eyes at the sound of her name. She thought she had dreamt it, but now she heard it again. It was Raoul, standing just outside the bedroom door, telling her there was a call for her. It had been transferred to her line; she could pick it up at her bedside phone. She thanked him, leaned over Bobby so as not to wake him, and picked up the receiver. Bobby, however, was already awake, sensitive as he was to the unlikely event of a phone call for his wife at seven in the morning.

It was Pam's aunt, Maggie Monahan, Jimmy Monahan's mother. "Pamela, it's your father," she said, choking back tears. Bobby watched as his wife's face suddenly became solemn. He could tell something was very wrong indeed.

Pam was sure her father was dead, but her aunt Maggie was quick to reassure her. Digger was in the hospital, but he was not dead. Not yet. As had happened so many times before, he had been picked up, half comatose, lying drunk in the street. Only this time he nearly died in earnest.

As Pam stared at the phone, she thought about Digger's chances. He was an old man now, and his years of drinking had aged him even more. Pam shuddered. This time or next could be the last time of all. It suddenly became clear to her: Digger was deliberately destroying himself—he was drinking himself to death with the purposefulness of a man bent on suicide.

Bobby sat up in bed, alert. He could tell without asking that something had happened to Digger. When he and Pam had been going out together, Digger had responded to their courtship by drinking himself into a stupor at least once a week. Their romance had been punctuated by visits to the emergency room. But this time Pam seemed more intense, more worried. Bobby guessed that it was because of what had happened at the barbeque not long ago. He knew that, to some degree, Pam blamed herself. If she hadn't joined herself by marriage to the hated Ewing clan, her father might still be among the ranks of the sober. It wasn't her fault, of course, but Bobby understood Pam's sense of guilt over her father's decline. He, too, began to get dressed.

As she went from closet to bedside, hurriedly getting herself together, rushing now to the bathroom to throw some cold water on her face, now to the dressing table to get her money and keys, she filled Bobby in on the details of Digger's latest brush with death. Then she noticed that he, too, was getting dressed.

"You don't have to come with me, Bobby. I'll be okay without you, and besides, Gary needs us here. At least one of us. Digger's not the only one who's having troubles."

Bobby was filled with love for his wife. In spite of her own family unhappiness, she had adopted his brother as part of her family and cared for his welfare like a true sister. Nevertheless, he insisted on accompanying her. He knew she wouldn't allow him to go inside the hospital with her, but the least he could do was drive her there. He knew the fastest route better than she did, and he felt sure he could make it back in time for breakfast. He would hardly be missed. Besides, Gary was doing just fine, he was sure. After last night's clearing of the air, he felt certain that his brother was over the hump and would have clear sailing from here on in. What could possibly go wrong, after all? Handing Pam her purse and stuffing the car keys into his front pocket, he ushered her out the door.

***

The breakfast crowd at Pete's had thinned out just a little, enough for Gary and Lucy to transfer to a booth. Pete had insisted they eat and insisted on treating them, too. He felt protective of his Valene. She'd worked for him for three years and had always been poor and alone. The first real happiness he had seen in her eyes was when Lucy had begun coming around; he wanted her to be happy. He felt like a father toward her, though he couldn't have said why. He had a family of his own, yet sometimes he felt closer to Val than to his own children. Maybe it was that his own children no longer needed him. At any rate, any friend of Val's was a friend of his, and he was damned if he'd let them come to his place and leave again without having a good breakfast.

They feasted on Pete's wonderful ham and egg special, with home fries and toast on the side, and a potful of coffee, while Val dealt with the rest of the breakfast traffic and cleaned up the dishes she had broken as best she could. She had refused Gary's and Lucy's offer of help, too embarrassed even to look at them, especially in front of her regular customers, who weren't used to her dropping things. This morning, she seemed to have come down with a regular plague of dropsies. Nothing as big as that first crash, but a slight spill here, and a dropped spoon there, until, as the crowd grew thinner, Pete mercifully relieved her of duty so that she could get cleaned up and spend some time with her visitors. Taking the tray from her, he began waiting on the remaining customers.

Thank God for Pete, thought Valene. She was sure she looked like a hurricane had hit her, and with barely a wave to Lucy and Gary, she headed for the restroom to do something about her appearance.

Meanwhile, Lucy and Gary sat over the remains of their breakfast, sipping the last of their coffee and talking about Val. In Lucy's expert opinion, Valene's butterfingers were a sure sign that she still cared about Gary. But Gary himself was less certain. As far as he was concerned, Val was just nervous, and she had every right to be. After all, it's not every day that a long-lost husband walks through the door after a sixteen-year absence!

He turned his gaze back to his daughter. "Since when have you been coming to meet your mother?" he asked. Lucy told him the story, punctuating it with concerned glances at Val, who had returned to the table, not sure she had done anything to fix her hair.

It hadn't been very long. A few months at most, although Lucy wasn't sure of the date. One day, coming out of school at the end of her day's classes, she'd noticed a blonde woman across the street staring in her direction. She hadn't paid her much attention, but when she got home, she couldn't get the woman out of her mind. When she had appeared a week later, and again the week after that, Lucy's interest had been piqued. She could not escape the feeling that the woman was somehow important to her life. Finally, she'd gone over to her and started a conversation. The truth had come out quickly, and her life had been different ever since. For the first time she felt a real meaning, a real mission in her life, and it had galvanized her into action. She'd cultivated the friendship of Jimmy Monahan and coerced him into driving her to Forth Worth every now and then. She and Val had been able to develop a deep friendship in just a short time. The visits hadn't been very long or very frequent, but they'd meant so much to Lucy, and she could tell that they meant just as much to Val.

Lucy had had only one question on her mind all morning, and now she felt she had to ask her father. "Daddy—Mama's going to come back to Southfork with us, right?"

Gary was taken aback. It had all been so sudden for him. Why, not three days ago he'd been just a lonely croupier at a Las Vegas hotel. Now he was back in the family fold, reunited with his wife and daughter, and his daughter wanted to know if her mother was going to come and live with them at the ranch! It was more than Gary could assimilate all at once, yet he tried to make sense of the situation for his daughter's sake as well as his own.

"I wouldn't get my hopes up, honey. I don't know whether it would be right for us to try to talk her into it, let alone whether she'd come." Lucy's face fell. Gary could see that, to Lucy, it was a life and death question, and he felt bad that he had seemed to brush it off. He hadn't meant it that way, but he knew that was what it sounded like to her.

Val finished what she was doing and made her way over to their table. "I'm not usually so clumsy," she apologized, sliding in next to Lucy on the red vinyl seat. Lucy interrupted her, however, saying she needed to use the bathroom. When Lucy had gone, Val smiled in embarrassment.

"What a surprise!" she exclaimed, nervously

touching her hair.

"Yes, it sure was—for me, too!" Gary agreed.

Val wondered aloud why he hadn't seemed more surprised when he'd seen her, and Gary explained to her that while Lucy hadn't said where they were headed, he'd put two and two together as they rode along in the truck, so that when they'd arrived, it was only half a shock to him.

Val was amazed to hear that Gary was staying at Southfork. She had been certain he'd never set foot there again after what had happened to him there. Gary related to her the circumstances under which he found himself back at the ranch. She found it hard to believe that he would have gone back; not that she couldn't understand his homesickness, but she felt that things couldn't have changed all that much from the time he'd run away.

Now she was amazed to hear him say, "You know, Val, you wouldn't believe it. Things are actually not bad over there. In fact, I'd say things are good! I'm flabbergasted about it. Even J.R. seems to have turned over a new leaf since I've been gone."

Val frowned. In spite of her dearest hopes, she couldn't bring herself to believe in J.R.'s reported transformation. No matter how much times goes by, she thought to herself, the leopard doesn't change his spots, nor does the devil grow a halo; to her, J.R. may as well have been the devil himself. However, she didn't want to put Gary off, or interfere with his seemingly good, optimistic mood, so she covered her frown and smiled at him happily.

Gary felt a warm rush going through him, the

same one he'd felt when she used to smile at him all those years ago. For a moment, it was as if no time had gone by at all. "You look great, Val," he heard himself saying.

Valene knew she was blushing, and to cover her embarrassment, she said, "Since when did you take up lying? You never used to lie; now, in the space of one minute, you start out by telling me J.R. has made an amazing transformation and wind up tellin' me how good I look after I've just got done with the breakfast shift and look like a greasy rag." Gary laughed. Same old Val, he thought, same wonderful, self-deprecating sense of humor.

"You know I'm not lying," he replied. Then, realizing that Lucy still hadn't come back, he added, "I think our daughter is trying to make a match of us." Valene nodded. The thought had occurred to her as well.

"You know," Gary continued, leaning in toward her, "nothing would please her more than for you to come back to Southfork with us."

Valene's face darkened, and her lips tightened. "I can't do that, Gary, no way in hell."

Gary looked at her carefully. Was it determination or just fear that was ruling her?

He tried again, taking a different tack. "Think how much it would mean to Lucy," he ventured.

Val shook her head. "He'd have my head if I showed up there and you know it."

Gary knew she meant J.R. There was no way to convince her of J.R.'s apparent transformation, but he felt he had to try.

"He's different now, Val, I feel sure of that."

Val looked deeply into his eyes. "Do you really

believe that, Gary?" she asked searchingly.

Gary nodded. "But even if I'm wrong," he went on, "there's no doubt about the way Mama and Daddy keep him in check. You should see it, Val, you'd be amazed."

Indeed she would, she thought. Lucy had told her about that aspect of it, how Pam had been accepted at Southfork over J.R.'s objections. Still...

Gary was quick to notice her wavering and jumped in. "Listen, Val, there's so much you and I have to talk over with each other. We can't get everthing said over breakfast. We need time together to sort it all out, the three of us, together. We could do that at the ranch..." Val sat silently, unable to move either way. "Please, Val," Gary said, "for Lucy and for me."

Before Val could answer, Lucy rejoined them and, as if she had been privy to the entire conversation, broke right in with, "Please, Mama, you just have to come back with us, you just have to!" Valene sat frozen in her chair, overwhelmed by the pressure being put on her by the two people who mattered most to her in the whole world.

After what seemed an eternity, Gary decided the issue for her. "Great, then it's decided. I'll call Mama and tell her to expect us." And with that he got up and headed for the phone.

Valene sat immobilized, but Lucy stopped Gary on his way out by saying, "Couldn't we just show up...make it a big surprise?"

Gary hesitated and looked at Val. She shook her head vigorously. It would be bad enough her just showing up, but to barge in without even a phone call! Gary caught the pleading look in her eye. "I better call, Lucy." Without giving her time to talk him out of it, he turned his back on his very persuasive daughter and his very frightened wife and walked away toward the telephones.

Lucy and her mother sat silently at the table. Lucy's heart was beating a mile a minute. It was the most exciting day of her life. She took her mother's hand and held it. Almost automatically, without being co scious of it, Val grabbed tightly onto the outstretched hand of her daughter as if it were a hand proffered to someone who was drowning.

In the backyard of the Southfork mansion, Raoul and Teresa were setting up for a big outdoor breakfast. It had been Miss Ellie's inspiration. She had always been a creative hostess, and she felt that it would serve as a more formal welcome for her boy than the hurriedly planned dinner of the night before. But Gary was nowhere to be found. Obviously, he and Lucy had gone off somewhere, but no one had any idea where. Ray Krebbs had reported that they'd taken his pickup a couple of hours earlier and gone off toward the main highway. But that was all anybody knew. Miss Ellie was a little worried. Not that she thought Gary was gone forever, but she didn't want him to miss the special surprise breakfast she had planned. Jock was sure that it was nothing to worry about, that they had probably gone off to see some old hangouts of either Lucy or Gary, and that they'd be back soon enough.

At that moment, Bobby and Pam ran downstairs and out of the house. Even from a distance it was evident to everyone in the backyard that Pamela was upset. She headed straight for the car while Bobby came over to explain where they were going and why they'd have to miss the special breakfast. As Pam opened the car door, she heard Jock's voice booming from the patio—"That Digger Barnes has done it again, huh?" Pam slammed the door and walked straight over to him. Ellie let out an audible gasp, horrified at her husband's lack of tact.

"That's right," said Pam, her voice in exaggerated control. "He's done it again, thanks to you! He came here to bury the hatchet with you, a man on the road to recovery, and you sent him reeling back into the gutter in just one short afternoon! Thanks to your kind treatment of him, he's back in the hospital, and he hasn't talked to me for weeks!"

She probably would have gone on, but by now Bobby had taken her by the arm and was leading her toward the car. "It's all right, Pammy, let's go." With a final furious stare at her shaken father-in-law, Pam spun on her heels, pulled her arm out of Bobby's grasp, and walked quickly over to the car.

There was silence in the backyard. Nobody moved until Pam's and Bobby's car was out of sight, and Raoul came out to tell them that Gary was on the phone. While Miss Ellie went inside to take the call, Sue Ellen put her arms around her father-in-law. If Pamela was going to be so hostile, Jock should know that he had at least one daughter-in-law who loved him and was loyal to the Ewing clan. But Jock was abashed. He knew he was at fault. He should have kept his mouth shut or, at least, spoken more quietly.

That damned voice of his carried so far, that was the trouble.

Miss Ellie re-emerged from the house and strode over to Jock. Both Jock and J.R. turned to look at her, wondering what the news was from Gary, and grateful to have the burden of Pam's anger put aside for the moment.

Ellie's face wore a look of complete shock. "I just spoke with Gary," she said to Jock, unnecessarily. "He and Lucy are... they..."

"Well, what is it, Ellie, spit it out," said Jock.

"They're with Lucy's mother!" she said, sitting down in a lawn chair.

J.R. nearly exploded. "What did you say?" he asked, not believing his ears. It was impossible. He had been so sure he was rid of her for good! Sue Ellen wanted to know how they had found her, and Ellie tried as best she could, from the little information Gary had given her over the phone, to answer everyone's questions.

"Lucy ran into her at school, Gary says, and they've been meeting regularly for quite some time," said Ellie, still a bit dizzy from all the new developments.

J.R. went over to his mama and put his arms around her protectively. "Don't you worry, Mama. We got rid of her once and we'll get rid of her again. Just give us a little time."

Ellie shook her head. "You don't understand, J.R. They're coming here. Right now. The three of them. I told them it was all right to bring her."

"Ellie!" Jock cried, shocked. He had no love for the trashy girl who he felt had ruined his son's life, but apparently his wife was ready to go to any lengths to make her son happy.

J.R. could feel the blood rising in his neck, his blood vessels distending with anger. Hadn't he told that girl to get out of the state and stay out forever? Nobody messed with J.R. Ewing that way and got away with it! Nobody!

Jock could feel his son's anger without J.R.'s saying a word, and he moved quickly to deflect it in spite of his own feelings. He wanted more than anything for Miss Ellie to be happy, and he knew he had to rein in this son if he were to protect Gary. "It's been a long time since we knew her, J.R. A lot has changed."

"But Daddy—trash is trash! We can't let her back here! Think of Lucy! Do you want her to be exposed to that element after we've worked so hard to erase it from her memory?"

Ellie felt the need to stand up for her weaker son, and for that poor girl, too. After all, she had nobody... "It's only for the day, J.R. Let's not ruin Gary's homecoming by being hostile to his wife—she is Lucy's mother, after all..."

J.R. winced. He hated to be reminded of his niece's lowly origins.

Jock had made up his mind. From the time he had spent with Gary the night before, he was convinced that the boy knew what he was now doing, and if he wanted to bring that girl back into his life, and to bring her over to see them, too, well, he could be big about it and allow her to visit. He was far from sure, but he was willing to take a chance. "I suppose it'll be all right," he said softly.

Miss Ellie felt that now was the time to clear up another sore point. "Thank you, Jock," she said, and then, turning to the family at large, she added, "I've been doing a lot of thinking about it, and

I've decided I want Gary to stay here at Southfork permanently.''

Everyone held his breath. They had all known this might happen, but still it came as a shock to all of them. "I was under the impression this was only a visit,'' Sue Ellen piped up, trying to be tactful.

Miss Ellie took her hand. "Yes, it was,'' she said soothingly, "but I want him to stay; I want my whole family with me...all my boys...I've missed him so much, and I'd be heartbroken if he went away again.'' Turning to Jock, she warned, "I won't stand for him being driven off again. Please, Jock, make him welcome.''

J.R. felt he had to say something. "Mama ...if Gary's getting back together with that awful girl, and even bringing her around here again, he can't have much sense, can he?''

But Jock stepped in, taking his boy by both shoulders and backing him away from his mother. "J.R., you heard your mother, now that's all there is to it. Gary's staying, and I don't want you interfering.''

Ellie saw that Jock was going to stand with her and keep J.R. in check, and she excused herself and went inside to give the two of them a chance to talk it out. When she had gone, Jock continued. "I don't know what you're cooking up in that head of yours, boy,'' he warned, "but shut off the fire right now.''

"I'm not cooking anything up,'' J.R. protested, but Jock wasn't buying that. He knew his son better than anybody, and he knew him well enough to know that J.R.'s schemes were nipped in the bud or not nipped at all.

"You've been acting like somebody's about to

take all your toys away from you. You know there's enough for everybody in this family, so stop hoarding what you've got, and open up to the others."

J.R. felt he had to stand up for himself. "It seems to me," he retorted, "that the business—the *family* business—has been doing rather well since you put me in charge. I don't see as you've got any cause for complaint with me."

"I don't care about making any more money," Jock persisted, his temper rising. "I've already lost one grandchild; I don't want to lose another." J.R. knew exactly what his father was referring to, and the reference stung him to the quick. His father, deep in his heart, blamed J.R. for Pamela's miscarriage. J.R. was innocent, of course. He hadn't pushed her out of that hayloft, she'd fallen. And if Bobby hadn't upset him so much that they'd had it out tooth and nail, she wouldn't have been so frightened and probably wouldn't have climbed up there in the first place. If he'd been drunk, it was because Bobby'd upset him, so he couldn't be blamed for the catastrophe.

"That's not fair! You can't blame J.R. for that!" said Sue Ellen, rushing to her husband's defense. But J.R. stopped her.

"Let him say his piece, darlin'," he said, deferring to his father in spite of his hurt feelings.

"Truth is, J.R., your stock seems to be going down. If you keep making trouble in this family, I promise you I'll take you right out of your chair at Ewing Oil and put Bobby in your place!" Jock turned to walk away, when an amusing thought struck him. Turning back to J.R. and Sue Ellen he said, "I might even put Gary in that chair!

Who knows?" And, with a laugh, he went into the house, his anger spent, his piece spoken.

He left behind him a chastened Sue Ellen and a shaken J.R. She turned to him helplessly, waiting for his reaction, expecting him to explode with anger. But, curiously, he was as calm as she had ever seen him—frighteningly calm. "My daddy just slapped my hand," he said evenly.

"What do you plan to do about it?" she asked.

He turned to her as if she should have already known the answer. "Why, Sue Ellen, don't you know? I'm going to do just what my daddy would like me to do. I'm going to be my brother's keeper, just like my daddy wants." And, with a peaceful, satisfied smile, he turned away confidently and strode into the house, leaving behind him a puzzled, confused Sue Ellen.

Chapter Eight

As Bobby escorted Pam into the lobby, he felt more than a little ashamed. He knew what kind of hospital this was. It was a hospital for people who could not afford to pay for their own medical care. Those who have lost their balance on the high wire of life and find themselves tumbling down, down, until they are rescued by the safety net of the state. Only those doctors who cannot go elsewhere were here. It had its very own kind of forlorn look and smell.

He wished he could buy Digger Barnes the best of medical care. He could have afforded to but, of course, Digger would never have accepted, not from a Ewing, not even from his daughter. Pam, too, felt the shame of her father's being in such a place. It seemed to her to symbolize how low he had fallen in the last few years, how hopeless his condition was, and how much distance had come between them. The guilt of it was almost more than she could bear. Turning to Bobby, she said, "Please—I'll find my own way home. Please, just go now, all right?" She couldn't stand for him to see her father in the condition she knew he would be in. Bobby, sensing his wife's discomfort, did not fight her. Kissing her on the cheek, he turned and went back out the door.

Upon learning the whereabouts of her father at the information desk in the lobby, Pam took the elevator up to the fourth floor. The car was dirty and slow. Surrounding her everywhere were the sick, the lame, the hopeless, people for whom life was an unrelieved agony. She could not help shuddering with revulsion at some of them.

Near the door to the detoxification ward sat her aunt, Maggie Monahan, a tired looking woman of sixty who might as well have been ten years older. She had taken care of Digger the past few years, as well as her son Jimmy, all on her meager salary. She had been through more than one ordeal, but to her credit, she knew how to take suffering. She didn't burden others with her troubles any more than was necessary, and she kept as optimistic an attitude as she could, mostly for her son's sake.

Pam hugged her tightly. But instead of greeting her warmly, Maggie told her she shouldn't have come at all. Pam protested that she had to see her father, but Maggie begged her not to. She knew what kind of a shock it would give Pam to see her father in this condition. She also knew that Digger had been unfair to Pam, making her life much harder by his bitter opposition to her marriage and by his refusal to speak to her or have anything to do with her. She could see how hurt Pam had been by his behavior, and how she still wanted his love,

118

and she tried to spare Pam the pain of another rejection. But Pam insisted on seeing the old man. Even if he cared nothing about himself, Pam still cared about him, and she was going to tell him so whether he could hear her or not.

Bracing herself, Pam pushed open the door of the ward. Instantly she was hit by the smell—the hideous, vile smell—and by the terrifying sounds of men and women living through a nightmare. The drug-crazed, the delirious, the tortured victims of self-abuse were all about her, crying, screaming, shivering, convulsing, twisting into the most impossible positions, squirming in pain and fear, calling out for help that would not come, wrestling with demons. Crammed together, yet hopelessly, completely alone.

In the far corner of the ward Pam saw her father. Barely recognizable, his chest heaved spasmodically, his body shuddered with the spasms of the D.T.'s. Sobbing, Pam went to his bedside and looked at the pitiful wreck of the man who was still her father. Maggie had told her he was out of the woods, at least for now. For now—but for how long? How long would it be before his bitterness at the Ewings and his disgust at himself would drive him off the deep end again, this time for good?

She leaned over him, and through her sobs said, "Daddy? Daddy, it's me—Pam. Oh, Daddy, I'm so sorry!" It was the truth. The guilt had overwhelmed her, and she stood there sobbing uncontrollably, the weight of the world on her shoulders, wishing she had never been born to cause him so much pain.

***

As they approached the big wrought-iron gate that was the entrance to Southfork Ranch, Val asked Gary to stop the truck and let her out. She stepped down and walked over to the arch for a better look at the mansion which topped the far horizon. There it was, the scene of the worst disaster of her life, the event that had changed her course as surely as a hurricane changes the course of a ship, changing her destiny with all the finality of an act of God. In her case, it had not been an act of God, but of man, which had sent her life reeling off into uncharted waters.

Gary stood beside her, gazing out at the ranch and then at Val.

"I'm not sure I can go ahead with it," Val said softly. "To look at it, it's so calm, so beautiful. It's hard to believe that your daddy and J.R. are waitin' for us over there."

Gary again tried to reassure her, telling her how Jock and Ellie seemed to have got the better of J.R., and how forthcoming J.R. had been upon his arrival. It seemed to him that things had truly changed in the Ewing family.

Lucy came down from the truck and joined the conversation. She, too, was sure it would be all right, that the family was so happy to have Gary back that they wouldn't jeopardize it by being hostile to Val. She reminded her mother about Pam's success in joining the family, but Val did not seem convinced. In her mind, she remembered J.R. as someone who said one thing but did another. If he hadn't bothered Pam, it was probably because she had a strong husband behind her backing her all the way, protecting her from J.R.'s machinations. Was Gary strong enough to protect her? She wondered.

Gary read her thoughts. "I know what you're thinking, Val, and I know it doesn't really change anything, but when I ran away that time, I had no idea they'd chase you away, too. If I had, I'd never have left without you." Val nodded. She believed him. Gary had too good a heart for that, weak as he may have been. She understood how he'd felt. "I was planning to come back," he said. "But I couldn't stay any longer. I was suffocating here. I had to go somewhere...anywhere but here. I would have taken you with me, but to where? For what? I was good for nothing, as far as I could see then."

Val held him tight. "Oh, Gary, that was just what J.R. told you about yourself—and you believed him!"

Gary had to agree—J.R. was his big brother, and he hadn't known then how to make up his own mind about things.

Now, for the first time, Val told him how J.R. had sent his thugs after her to take Lucy away. What could she have done? At least she'd trusted Miss Ellie to bring Lucy up right.

They both looked at Lucy, at the fine young woman she'd become, and, while they could see Miss Ellie had done well with her, the pain of not having been able to raise her themselves shot through both of them at once. If only they could be together now...a family...

"By the way," said Gary, "I forgot to ask you ...have you gotten married again?" Val shook her head, and looked up inquiringly at Gary. "Me neither," he said. Holding each other's hands, the three of them got back into the truck and drove on to the ranch.

***

When they heard the truck coming down the entrance road, the family got up from their seats on the patio to greet the arrivals. Bobby had made it back from the hospital in time. As Val emerged from the truck, her eyes met J.R.'s, and they held each other's gaze for a moment. In Val's eyes there was genuine fear, as if she had committed some colossal offense by coming back to Southfork and was awaiting punishment for her misdeed. But in J.R.'s eyes, there was nothing readable at all—if he felt hostility toward her, he hid it well. He strode over to her directly and took her hand in his. With all her being she strove not to pull her hand out of his grasp. She had to give him the benefit of the doubt, no matter what her instincts told her.

"Why, Valene," said J.R., a wide, warm smile on his face, "you look as young as the last time I saw you." Valene thanked him for the compliment. At least on the surface J.R. was going to be friendly to her. That made it a bit easier. "You remember Miss Ellie...and I'd like you to meet my wife..., Sue Ellen, this here's Valene Clements..." Sue Ellen smiled her brightest stewardess smile, a smile which never quite seemed to reach her eyes, and greeted the newcomer as warmly as she could manage. "And here's brother Bobby," continued J.R., "all grown up."

Valene smiled at Bobby, and she could see that at least one of the Ewings was genuinely glad to see her back at Southfork. Bobby hugged her. "We're so glad to have you here, Val—it makes Gary's return even better—a real homecoming!"

Val thanked him and then, noticing Bobby was alone, asked after his wife, whom she really wanted to meet. Pam would be a real friendship possibility, she felt, since the two of them were both outsiders. Bobby explained about Pam's visit to the hospital. It appeared there were other problems going on at the ranch besides hers and Gary's. Somehow it gave Valene a sense of relief to think that the focus wasn't entirely on her.

Jock greeted her next, a little stiffly, but trying his best. He shook her hand hard, the only way he knew how, and then, to cut short the embarrassment of first greetings he said, "Hey, here we are all standing while the food's getting cold! Miss Ellie made a real Texas breakfast—we can't just let it go to waste!" Val, for one, was starved. Lucy and Gary had eaten, but she had worked right through breakfast, and her nervousness had kept her from feeling her hunger till now.

As they walked toward the patio where the food was waiting for them, still simmering over the sterno pots, J.R. took Valene by the arm so that they trailed the others by a few feet. As they walked, he said to her softly, privately, but just loud enough for the others to hear: "Val, honey, me and Gary have been getting reacquainted— getting to be real brothers again, burying the past, so to speak. I hope you and I can bury the old hatchet, too."

Val felt a wave of uneasiness sweep over her. She felt confused by J.R.'s overwhelming friendliness; one thing was for sure—she didn't trust it. "Hey, why not?" she said, uncertainly. Could he really have changed toward her? And if he hadn't, for whose benefit was he acting so warmly?

"We were all so foolish and willful in those days," he explained, holding her by the arm all the while, "nobody more than me. But now we're all older and wiser, and I hope we can leave the past behind us, hmmm?" And without waiting for her to answer him, he strode over to Gary, who was taking just enough food to be polite. "Gar, could I have a word with you?" Gary put down his plate and allowed himself to be led away from the table by his older brother. Valene watched, more and more confused and curious.

When they were out of earshot, J.R. turned to his brother and said his piece. "Gary, I guess you know that Mama intends for you to stay here with us for good." Gary started to protest, but J.R. continued, putting his hand up in the air for silence. "I know how that must make you feel...here you've taken such a big step, coming back here even for a visit, and right away we're putting the pressure on you to stay. You don't know if you're up for rejoining the family, and that's perfectly all right. These things take time. Still...you know what it would do to Mama if you went away again now."

It was unbelievable. J.R. was asking him to stay. The very same brother who had almost single-handedly driven him away back then! But he knew J.R. was right—Miss Ellie had pinned all her hopes on him. And the thought oppressed him—he was barely strong enough to bear the weight of his own life, let alone the hopes of his mother and Lucy. "Maybe if I got a place not far away, J.R.," he suggested hopefully. The solution had occurred to him on the way to the ranch with Valene and Lucy. But J.R. was shaking his head, frowning.

"You've said that before, Gary, and look what happened."

It was true. When he'd run away, he'd thought at first he'd stay nearby, but halfway solutions never worked, he had found, and now J.R. was reminding him of it.

As if to cement his brother's resolve, J.R. added, "If it makes any difference in your mind, I want you to know that it's not only Mama...I also want you to stay." Gary looked away from his brother, abashed. Maybe Bobby had been right when he'd said J.R. wasn't so bad after all. He gazed out at the ranch, the land he loved with all his heart. It made a great deal of difference that J.R. wanted him to stay—the decisive difference, in fact.

J.R. saw his brother looking out at the land, and guessed accurately what he was thinking. "We'll find something useful for you to do, little brother, don't you worry about that. I know you'd prefer the land and maybe that's the place for you, but you know we're into all kinds of things these days—gotta diversify if you want to stay competitive, I always say!"

Gary laughed with him. He felt like saying, 'good old J.R.,' but somehow 'good old' was an unfamiliar way of looking at his brother.

Again, J.R. could sense that his brother was wavering, and before Gary had a chance to object or raise any doubts, he steered the discussion away by saying, "Hey—our food's gettin' cold! Let's go get us some—we'll talk about this later. There's plenty of time, after all—plenty of time!" And slapping his brother on the back, he guided him back toward the patio.

Pamela could stand no more. She felt if she did not get out of the room, she would explode. Her body, racked with sobs, shook, convulsed with guilt and horror. She stood up and fled the room, nearly running, not looking where she was going, not even able to breathe until the doors of the ward were closed behind her and she was once again in the waiting room.

As she tried to calm down, breathing deeply and wiping her eyes with her handkerchief, her Aunt Maggie came out to join her, an apprehensive expression on her face. She had warned her niece not to go in to see Digger, but Pam had insisted. Now she had upset herself completely, and she hadn't done her father a bit of good. If only young people weren't so impetuous, she thought, and were a little more willing to take the advice of those a little older and wiser than themselves.

Pam, having gained control of herself, turned to her aunt. "Oh, Aunt Maggie, we've got to get him out of this awful place! Right this minute! I can't stand the thought of him being here!"

Maggie hugged her niece. "As soon as he's out of the woods, honey...can't rush these things."

Pam looked around her at the grimy walls and the hopeless wrecks of human beings everywhere. "But this place is a living hell!" she wailed.

"Yes, honey, I know," answered her aunt, "but Digger doesn't know that. He doesn't even see it."

Pam pulled away. "*I* see it, Aunt Maggie, and I can't stand it!"

Maggie frowned. She knew that she would have

126

to do some tough talking now. Her niece was so headstrong. Her impulses were kind and good, but her judgment was clouded by emotion, and she needed to be overruled by a cooler head. "Pamela, even if he were able to leave, you know he wouldn't go with you—not anywhere, not ever."

"But I'm his daughter!" Pam cried, the guilt overflowing in her, "I've got to do something for him!"

"He won't let you do anything for him!" Maggie shouted at her. "He's too bitter and too angry—and there's nothing you can do about it!"

Pam fell apart. The truth of her aunt's words shattered her as a hammer shatters glass, and, once again, she collapsed in tears. Maggie's heart, already so heavy with grief, went out to her niece. Her words had gotten through, and now it was time to sooth Pam with some words of hope. "I'll talk to him as soon as he's well enough to listen, honey. I'll do my best to get him to see you again. But, until then, you've got to stay far away from him. Let him heal, baby—he's hurt bad, and he's got to have time to mend."

Pam shook her head obstinately. She couldn't stay away from her father—he needed her whether he knew it or not. She started to protest, but her aunt stopped her. "Please Pam! Stop thinking of yourself! Whatever your needs are, it's what he needs that matters now."

There was nothing Pam could say. Her aunt was right and she knew it. Bowing her head, she nodded in agreement, feeling that she might never see her father again, knowing he wanted it that way. Overwhelmed with sadness, she let her aunt lead her out of the hospital, out into the fresh, healthy air.

Chapter Nine

Gary shielded his eyes from the fierce afternoon sun as he looked out at the seemingly endless rangeland. For as far as the eye could see, cattle grazed or sat under the trees swishing away the flies with their tails. Birds flew lazily in the sky overhead, and a breeze hissed in the tall meadow grass.

A jeep carrying Ray Krebbs pulled up beside Gary. It was the first time the two men had met— Lucy had gotten the truck from Ray herself that morning, while Gary waited by the stables. Gary looked at the ranch foreman closely. He knew that his daughter liked him enormously and that the two were close friends. He could see why. Ray Krebbs exuded likeability. He instinctively impressed Gary as warm, loyal, and extremely capable. Jock Ewing had chosen well when he'd entrusted the ranch to this man, Gary decided. The two shook hands warmly.

"Pleased to meet you," Ray began. "J.R. told

me to treat you like royalty. He said you'd be staying permanently, and for me to give you the complete tour."

Gary felt momentarily out of control. They were taking his destiny out of his hands. "I haven't decided yet whether I'll be staying, but I'd appreciate the tour, thank you."

Hopping into the jeep with Ray, Gary soon found himself riding over the land he loved. Southfork seemed to go on forever in every direction as far as a person could see. "This was always what I loved best," he confided in Ray. "The oil business always left me cold, frankly."

Ray nodded in agreement. He liked Gary right away. This Ewing was a man like himself. "I try my best to stay on top of all the new equipment and techniques," he said proudly. "Since Jock got interested in the cattle, he's spared no expense to make this the showplace of Texas ranching."

Gary could see that it was true. The ranch was as well run as a ranch could be. But instead of giving him a sense of familial pride, it somehow left him with an empty, even worried feeling.

"So we're doing well, then, with the ranching end?" he asked off-handedly.

"Yep," answered Ray, smiling.

Looking around him, Gary noticed the emptiness of it all. "But it looks like, with all the land we've got, we could be raising five, six times as many head of cattle as we do!" he offered, hopefully.

Ray nodded knowingly. "That's true enough, but there'd be no point. See, the government pays us subsidies *not* to raise them. Crazy, huh? But that's the way it is."

Gary's heart sank. It was obvious that Ray and his father had things well in hand and that there was no prospect for growth. He would be a third wheel—there was no need for him on the ranch.

Seeing Gary's displeased expression and mistaking it for skepticism, Ray offered to let Gary look at the books. He waved Ray off; he believed him implicitly. "You and Dad must be pretty busy with the ranch, huh?" he asked, knowing the answer already in his heart.

"To be honest with you, I could oversee the whole place by myself, but since Jock gets such a kick out of it all, we do it together." Having arrived back where they'd begun, Ray stopped the jeep to let off his passenger.

"Ray, thanks for the tour. I really appreciate your taking the time."

"Hey, look," offered Ray, feeling instinctively what Gary was going through. "If you'd like to help out, I'm sure we can find enough for you to do."

But Gary knew the difference between kindness and truthfulness. Nodding his head diffidently, he thanked Ray and walked off toward the stables where Val and Lucy sat outside talking. Waving goodbye, Ray got back in the jeep and rode off.

Lucy was smiling conspiratorially as Gary approached them, while Valene had an embarrassed look on her face. "What's going on here?" said Gary cheerfully, masking his disappointment at not being needed at the ranch.

"I was just explaining to Mama," said Lucy, "that you two are still in love with each other! You must be! Why else haven't either of you gotten married again?"

Valene studied the ground hard as if there were something down there of great interest to her. Gary tried to deflect her embarrassment. "Lucy, any torch I'd been carrying would have incinerated me ten times over—alcohol is flammable, you know!"

They all laughed, grateful to have the topic lightened. Still, Lucy felt they ought to be discussing their future together. After all the years she'd waited, she didn't have the patience to wait any longer. Val and Gary tried to calm her down. They both still felt strongly for one another, but so much had happened so fast that they felt they needed time to grow into the changes. They had jumped into marriage once before, and it had turned out to be a disaster, despite the depth of their love for each other. Now there were other factors to be considered. . .

As if in response to their deepest anxieties, a jeep bounded across the range in their direction, J.R. at the wheel. In the passenger seat sat Ray Krebbs. J.R. pulled up to the front of the stables, and Ray got out. With a look at them, Lucy turned back to the subject at hand.

"We can stay close now and get to know each other for real!" Gary nodded at her, but he was staring over at the two men. "What did you find out from Ray?" Lucy wanted to know.

"Everything I needed to know. There's no room for me running the ranch, honey. He and Grandpa have the place well in hand."

Lucy caught the tone in his voice. "Daddy, you are going to settle down here now, aren't you?" The fear was audible in her voice. Gary would have liked to reassure her, but he didn't want to mislead her.

"I don't know, baby. . .we'll see. . .maybe it'd be better for me someplace else. . ."

Lucy felt the panic rising inside of her. Without any control over what she was saying, she blurted out, "Why don't you just fire Ray and take over the ranch yourself? He's not that important, and I'm sure you could do a better job of it. . ."

Gary was shocked at her betrayal of a close friend out of her desperation to keep him with her.

"That's enough now, Lucy! I don't want to hear another word against Ray Krebbs, do you hear me?"

Lucy hung her head, ashamed. She knew she'd said something terrible, but what choice did she have? She needed her father back, more than anything—more, even, than friendship.

Val tried to soothe her daughter. "Don't press your daddy, baby." Lucy nodded, and Val put her arms around her.

J.R. left Ray and pulled up beside them. As he strode over to them, Val felt herself stepping backwards, away from him. But J.R. had a big smile on his face, and he went right up to her. "How are you all doin'?" he inquired, putting his hand on her shoulder. "Havin' a good time?"

"Sure are!" said Gary, as happy as he could manage to sound.

"That's real good—I'm glad about that. And I want you to keep on havin' a good time indefinitely!" Then he laughed. "Listen to me— giving a Ewing permission to have a good time on Ewing land!" He seemed to find the idea enormously amusing. Then he turned serious.

"Oh, by the way...I've been doing a lot of thinking, Gary, about you staying around, and I had a terrific idea—such a good idea that I had to come right out here and tell you about it!"

Lucy stood up, her hopes reviving. Maybe J.R., the unlikeliest of people, would wind up being the one who convinced her father to stay. "What's the idea? Let's hear it!" she said cheerfully.

J.R. squatted down, being careful not to dirty his suit with the dust of the ranch. "Well, now and then, we—Ewing Oil, that is—like to pick up little companies we think we can make winners out of, and there's one we took over not long ago that's just a gem. It deals with petroleum by-products, you know, the waste that's left over when the refining's done. It's been making a nice steady profit, but we've only had time to operate it at, oh, five, ten percent capacity. I thought it might be perfect for you to take over and run with. There's a lot of money in that gook, you know! And you'd be doing something really useful!"

Gary squinted his eyes. "You really think that's the sort of thing I could handle?" he asked doubtfully.

"Definitely! No doubt about it!" J.R. reassured him. "This is a sure thing operation. All it needs is a little common sense and a little money in the right places, and that nice little profit will turn into a huge bonanza, mark my words!"

"I don't know, J.R. I really don't know anything about the oil business...I was thinking of working on the ranch...*if* I stayed..."

J.R. stood up. "But you can see for yourself that the ranch is all taken care of. Didn't Ray tell you?"

Gary nodded. "Yes, that's true enough..."

J.R. jumped right back in. "Now, this company's a cinch to learn about, believe me. Just needs a little new machinery, and all you have to do is increase its operations, little by little—just more of the same, nothing different. And Daddy'n me would be there if you needed us. What do you say?"

Gary hesitated. "I just don't know, J.R. I will give it some thought. And I do appreciate the offer. But..."

J.R. didn't give him time to finish. "Good! Good man! You give it some thought, and I'm sure you'll take me up on it—it's too good an offer to miss!" And with a pat on the back for Gary, he turned and headed back for the jeep.

Lucy got up and ran after him. "Wait up, J.R.—I'm coming back with you."

J.R. arched his eyebrows. "Just us?" he asked, a hint of humorous skepticism in his voice. "Think we can trust these two turtle doves alone?"

Lucy smiled. "No, I don't," she answered knowingly, "that's why I'm coming with you." And, winking at her uncle, she hopped into the jeep beside him and they drove off toward the house.

As the jeep drove out of sight, Val turned to Gary, her hand on his knee. Her face was full of trouble. She felt, deep down inside of her, that something was wrong with all this, but Gary's and Lucy's optimism and willingness to try again had won her over and brought her this far. She had returned to Southfork, a place she had never thought she'd see again, and had kept her fears and reservations pretty much to herself. All had seemed friendly enough, but somehow she felt it was all unreal.

She had played along, waiting for the storm to break. And now, at last, it had broken. She knew for certain, inside herself, although she had no proof to back it up, that nothing had changed—nothing at all. J.R. was still the same old J.R., and there was no future for her, or for Gary, at Southfork.

"Gary?" she began, not really knowing how to tell him of her fears.

"Hmmmm?" he turned to her, smiling. He wasn't at all sure that he could handle the company J.R. had offered him, but he felt optimistic—at least there might be someplace for him to fit in.

"Gary," she went on, "you've got to get out of here, right away."

Gary was completely taken aback. It was the last thing he had expected her to say. "What are you talking about, Val? Didn't you hear what J.R. said? Everything's going fine!" He affected a bit more enthusiasm than he really felt to counter what he felt was her unreasonable fear.

But Val was adamant. "I heard what he said, all right. Now you listen to what I'm telling you. Get your bags packed right away. Right now. And head on out of here. Go to California, or somewhere far away from here. I'll come out too, maybe after a little while...we'll call each other every few days, stay in touch...if it all works out and I come out to join you, we can send for Lucy too, be a family again—if that's what you want," she added.

Her urgency caught him off guard. "Wait just a second, Val...what's gotten into you? I don't understand why you're acting like this."

"It's J.R., Gary. He's after you again. He's

going to run you out of here just like he did before.''

Gary was incredulous. J.R. had been as friendly as he could be, and this was how Val reacted to it! ''Now, hold on a second, honey, give J.R. a chance—''

Val shook her head vehemently. ''He's up to something, I know it. I feel it in my bones. I don't know what it is, but whatever it is, you're going to wind up a wreck, tossed out in the trash and thrown away, just like before. And once he's gotten rid of you, it'll be my turn...Lucy'll be alone again—more alone than ever.''

Having said her piece, she got up and started walking back toward the house leaving Gary behind, more confused than he had ever been before. Could Val be right? Was it possible? He shook his head in wonderment. Why was everything so impossibly complicated?

Chapter Ten

By the time the taxi dropped Pam at Southfork, she had calmed down somewhat. Her visit to the hospital had shaken her composure. What had really gotten to her was her Aunt Maggie's order to stay away—from her own father! It made her feel as if she was poison and the feeling was almost more than she could bear.

On her arrival she went straight up to her room and told Bobby the whole story. He listened quietly, but there was little he could say to make her feel better. He assured her that Digger would be all right, but Pamela knew that the old man's body couldn't take much more abuse. Besides, he was ruining her Aunt Maggie's life as well as his own. She felt she ought to be there, to take some of the burden on herself. Bobby wished there was something he could do, but neither he nor Pam could imagine what that would be. Gently, he suggested that they go downstairs so that Pam could meet Valene. Pam agreed reluctantly but her mind was back at the hospital.

"Oh, Bobby, he didn't even know who I was!" she moaned.

On the patio, Lucy, Gary and Val were sipping cold drinks. Lucy hurried to introduce Pam and Valene. Pam did her best to raise a smile, apologizing for not being there to greet her when Val arrived. Val asked after Pam's father. Pam only said that he was very sick. She didn't want to burden anyone else with her problems.

Lucy was so excited about the job J.R. had offered her father that she launched right into telling Pam all about it. Gary tried to stop her, saying it was too soon to be bragging about something he hadn't even decided to accept. But Lucy was determined.

Pam was in no frame of mind to hear about anybody's good news. She suddenly felt overwhelmed with guilt and worry. This was not the place for her right now. She had to be with her father, whether he wanted her there or not. Hurriedly excusing herself, she ran toward the driveway. Bobby ran after her.

"Hey, don't you want to hear about Gary's new business opportunity?"

"I'll hear about it later. I have to go to my daddy now."

"But Pam," Bobby called after her, "I thought you said Aunt Maggie said to stay away!"

"She's going to take him back to her house, Bobby—I've got to see him, no matter what Aunt Maggie says!"

And without another word, she was gone, leaving a worried, puzzled Bobby behind.

***

As Bobby returned to the patio, he saw that J.R. was already standing there, a huge pile of folders in his arms and a big smile on his face. "Gary, how 'bout you and I go into the house and get started going over this stuff?"

Gary looked at Valene. It was a huge amount of material. She looked away from him, having already said her piece and not wanting J.R. to know how she felt about things. Slightly miffed, Gary got up without a word and followed J.R. inside.

Bobby went over to Val. "I think I'll go join those two and make sure Gary's okay." Val didn't say a word, but there was gratitude in her eyes. How had the Ewings managed to produce both J.R. and Bobby?

Lucy put her arms around her mother. "Don't worry, Mama. Daddy's gonna be great at this new business. You wait and see." But Val was worried. Very worried indeed.

In the small study, J.R. and Gary sat behind the mahogany desk, their heads invisible from the other side of the room because of the immense stack of papers which covered the entire surface. Standing behind Gary's chair was Bobby, watchful for any sign of trouble, but anxious for everything to go well.

J.R. was laying it all out for Gary. "The bulk of the stuff you'll have to read through is over at the Ewing Oil building downtown, but you can get started on this. It's pretty easy reading for this kind of stuff, and I thought you should look through it before we sat down with the lawyers to finalize things."

Suddenly Gary felt his head spinning. He felt as if he were buried underneath all the papers—papers which might as well have been written in another language. He felt as out of place as a penguin in the Sahara, and the mention of the word lawyers was enough to send a shudder through his body. He wished this roller coaster would slow down long enough for him to catch his breath, but he knew the ride had just begun. He felt what little confidence he had crumbling inside of him.

Bobby leaned over him. "Don't worry about the lawyers, Gar...J.R. did the same thing when I joined Ewing Oil. It's just part of the way these things are done. You'll get used to it soon enough."

"Hey, listen," rejoined J.R., "we've got lots of time for all this—there's no need to rush. And Gary, you know there's no need for you to go ahead with this if you don't want to. Don't feel obligated. I just want to bring the lawyers in to explain the whole thing to you. That'll make it easier for you to decide if this business is for you." He put his arm around his brother affectionately. "I let Mama know I was offering you this opportunity," he added off-handedly. The point behind his words was not lost on Gary. "Let me tell you, brother, it would make her very happy to know you were involved in the family business like this...you do want to make her happy, of course..." He paused to let the thought sink in. "'Course, you have to make up your own mind what's best for you...You just take your time going over these things...I'll be back later to see how you're getting on." He smiled and patted

Gary on the back. Motioning Bobby to follow him out of the room, they left Gary sitting there, dwarfed by the pile of folders in front of him, a very small ship tossed on a very large ocean.

The Monahan house was a small, modest one, in a poor but respectable neighborhood of working class homes. The house itself was well-kept, immaculately clean, but the cleanliness did little to make up for the old, thread-bare furniture which lined the walls. As Pam drove into the driveway, she remembered it as it had been when she was growing up. It had seemed much bigger then, and she remembered it having always had a fresh coat of paint. Those were the days when Digger was still earning a decent living.

Pam couldn't help reflecting on the huge difference between this poor little house, and the huge mansion where she now resided. If only she could use some of that wealth to help these people! But she knew they would never allow that. Although they were poor, they were also proud. Pam, herself, would never have accepted charity either back in the days before she'd met Bobby.

Aunt Maggie sat in her old armchair, bone weary from her ordeal. At last she could get a little rest. Digger was asleep, and Jimmy had just gone off to work for the night. Her eyes were almost closed when the knock at the door came.

Pam stood facing her aunt, a determined expression on her face. "I know what you told me," she began immediately, "but I couldn't stay away." She kissed her aunt and went past her into the house, without waiting for the invitation she knew would not be coming. "How is he doing?"

she asked, dropping her bag onto a chair.

"He's asleep," Maggie answered. She noticed the bag. "What have you got in there?" she pointed.

"Oh, I went to the store on the way here. Some reading...puzzles, a few magazines, a book or two..."

Maggie stared at the bag. Her niece was ignoring the facts of the matter, and she was heading for a fall. She felt it her duty to warn her.

"He isn't going to be happy to see you, honey," she said, shaking her head sadly.

"Well, that's too bad, because I need to see him. Ever since he came to Southfork that day I've been trying to see him, but..."

"He's never given you the chance," Maggie finished her sentence for her.

"I don't even know if he knows about my miscarriage."

Maggie sighed. "Well, I told him about it, but it's hard to tell if he heard me or not. You never know with him if a thing registered or not."

Pam knew it was true. "But *why?* That's what I'd like to know. Why is he pushing me away like this? It's making me crazy!"

Maggie sat down next to her niece and took her hand in hers. "Well, baby, going to that barbeque at Southfork just brought everything home to him, you know. You being one of them...Jock being so rich and popular and well connected...in your daddy's mind, all those things were supposed to be his, and Jock stole them from him—you included. And then when Jock insulted him like that in front of everybody..." Pam felt the tears coming to her eyes, stinging her with the memory. "Your daddy always blamed Jock for everything bad that's happened in his life. That's only partly fair. Jock deserves some of the blame, but not everything was his fault..."

Pam nodded. It was true, but it didn't change a thing.

"But in your daddy's mind, the Ewings are the same as the devil. 'Jock Ewing stole everything I ever had!' he always said, and he believes it, too. You marrying Jock's son was about the final straw, I think."

Pam knew it was true. Her marriage had proved the truth of Digger's own mad imaginings. She knew he was down the hall a few steps in the room where he had always slept, right next to hers. The stairs suddenly seemed long and menacing. "I've always loved this place," she mused. "You brought me up, and Jimmy, and Cliff...and you took care of Daddy too, all in this one tiny little house...it's amazing how you did it all!"

Maggie chuckled softly. "Well, there's nothing amazing about it. For the most part, I actually enjoyed it." Then her face fell as her consciousness came back to the present moment. "Honey, you've got to go home... he's not nearly ready to see you yet...not by a long ways." Pam clenched her jaw defiantly and shook her head. Without a word, she got up and marched down the hall, her bag in hand. Maggie stared up after her, not moving to stop her, resigned to let fate take its course. There was a limit, after all, to any one person's strength.

Pam opened the door to her father's room and

was greeted immediately by the smell. It wasn't the ordinary kind of sweat, but the sweat perspired by someone with a fever, the sweat of a very sick man. He lay in his bed, curled up like a fetus, sleeping silently. He looked, if it were possible, even worse than he had looked in the hospital, more tired, more wasted. She stood over him, tears rolling down her cheeks. "Daddy?"

The blue, almost transparent eyelids fluttered and opened, and the red, swollen eyeballs stared up at her. "Hi, Daddy—it's me," she smiled.

The dry, cracked lips began to smile back at her. Suddenly, Digger's face hardened. Words that were unintelligible to Pam came out in a whisper. She leaned over and asked him to repeat himself. This time there was no mistaking either his words or his meaning. "Get out of here," Digger said.

Pam felt her composure cracking. "But, Daddy..."

"You're still a Ewing, ain't you?" he croaked.

"Daddy, won't you listen to me?" she begged, close to breaking down.

"If you're still a Ewing, you have nothing to say to me." He closed his eyes, and his mouth hardened into a frown.

"Please, Daddy, can't you give me a chance?" she whispered, her voice choked by sobs.

"I did give you a chance. I went with you— there. Same old Jock Ewing—did it to me all over again..."

"Oh, Daddy, I know, please forgive me for bringing you there, it was a terrible mistake...but I love Bobby...he's my husband...I can't help it if he's a Ewing! What can I do about it?" Pam was near hysterics.

Digger, though deathly weak, was filled with a rage that propelled him to drive away the person dearest to him in the world. "Leave him, that's what. Jock Ewing did it to me again, and you just stood there and watched him! You're still living there, even after that! I don't understand you at all. And I don't want you around here, either!"

Pam was speechless. Her lips kept forming the word 'please' but she was sobbing so hard the words wouldn't come out.

"Get out of here," yelled Digger, his voice rising beyond his strength.

Pam shook her head obstinately. She would stay whether he wanted her to or not. Digger somehow summoned up a strength no one would have guessed was in him—the strength of his hatred for the Ewings, and he directed the full force of it at his daughter. "Get out of here!" he screamed, pushing himself up out of the bed, "Get out of my sight!" His arms flailed wildly about him, forcing Pam to retreat to the door. "I have no daughter, do you hear me? My daughter is dead! Dead, dead, dead!!!" And he slammed the door on his terrified daughter.

Pam was gone, and a wheezing, coughing Digger collapsed on the floor, his momentary strength gone from him, leaving only a weeping, woeful shell. "Dead...dead... dead..." he repeated senselessly. Despite his near-delirium, he realized that he had driven away the person he loved most in the entire world...his daughter was gone, and with her his only reason for living. He curled up into a ball, sobbing and rocked himself until he lost consciousness, falling mercifully asleep.

Chapter Eleven

Gary stood at the window of the study, one of the folders in his hands, staring out into space. He didn't know how long he'd been staring like that, but Bobby's voice brought him back to reality. His brother was standing in the doorway, smiling at him and shaking his head. "Hey, Gary, give it a break! You've been in here for three hours...what do you say we saddle up and go for a ride? How long has it been, anyway?"

"Longer than I care to admit."

Bobby smiled. "Think you still know one end of a horse from the other?"

Gary laughed, caught up in the spirit of fun, relieved to be distracted from the mountain of papers. "Do they still have to tie you into the saddle?"

"Hey!" said Bobby, raising his fists playfully, "put up your dukes!" The two of them set in to a mock fight, dancing around the table, throwing jabs and one-liners back and forth.

Gary completely forgot himself in the fun, for the first time since he'd been back, and was having a great time, when they were both brought up short by a voice saying, "How about a tag team match?" It was J.R., standing framed in the doorway, a disapproving look on his face.

Gary lowered his hands sheepishly. He felt he should apologize somehow, but Bobby stepped in for him.

"Give him a break, J.R. He's home only one day and already you've piled on the paper work! I came in to take him out riding—any objection to that?"

J.R. shrugged. "Not at all. Go right ahead...if that's what you want to do...I just thought Gary wanted to get started right away, that's all..."

"Hey," Bobby objected, again speaking up for his seemingly tongue-tied brother, "what's the big hurry? He's gonna be here for a long time."

Instead of answering directly, J.R. turned to Gary: "Bobby's used to life on the road—still got jet-lag, I'm afraid. Time is just a bubble to him..." And he laughed, as if to say, 'you and I, Gary, understand the importance of time.'

Ignoring the jibe, Bobby offered, "Well, Gar, shall I get the horses ready?" But J.R. had hit paydirt with Gary and he wasn't going to let the fish get off the hook now. Turning to Bobby, he took it upon himself to defend Gary against Bobby's 'bad influence.'

"Listen, Bobby, Gary's got a lot to catch up on. He wants to show his daughter he's somebody to look up to...and his wife, maybe, too...Valene's lookin' awfully good, and I think she still has a soft spot for him...there's a lot at stake for him. Isn't that right, Gary?"

Bobby was mad now. He could see what J.R. was trying to do. "I just want him to take an hour off...not a week!"

But it was too late. Gary put his hand up and said softly, "Bobby, maybe J.R. is right. I'd better take a rain check on that ride. There's too much work here for me to do." He reached for the folder he'd been trying to read and sat back down at the table. Bobby and J.R. looked at each other. Bobby was flushed with anger, but on J.R.'s face there was nothing but the deepest contentment.

In the kitchen, Val and Ellie were getting reacquainted. They sipped iced tea from a pitcher Ellie had prepared herself. It was her special recipe, and she pressed Val to drink lots of it. For her part, Val found herself more interested in the conversation. This woman had brought up her daughter and had done a wonderful job of it, for all she could tell.

"Lucy's so out front, so generous and good-hearted—I have you to thank, Miss Ellie."

Ellie laughed. "You've only seen the bright side of her," she said knowingly, "wait till you've been around for awhile. I'm sure you'll be treated to quite an array of behaviors. I'd say Lucy is a typical adolescent—romantic, adventurous, and more than a little temperamental. Of course, I would have loved to do some of the same things when I was her age, if times hadn't been so different..."

Val knew what Ellie meant. She, herself, hadn't had much opportunity to be adventurous. From the time she was little she'd always had to work. "I believe you, Miss Ellie, but she seems so perfect! I guess I'm prejudiced," she concluded.

"You'll get to know her better after a while," nodded the older woman.

Val tensed. "I don't know if I'll be able to—" she meant to say "stay here," but Miss Ellie misconstrued her meaning.

"Sure you will. You'll be a perfectly good mother. There are things that she and I can never share, as much as we love each other."

Val let it go at that. She couldn't seem to come out and say what she felt. "I wonder about Gary..." she began. But, in her happiness, Miss Ellie again misunderstood Val's meaning.

"He's crazy about you, honey, I can tell that a mile away."

Val smiled. "Thanks, Miss Ellie. But that's not what I meant. You see, I don't know if being at Southfork is good for him."

Miss Ellie looked up in surprise. "Why of course it is! This is his home — he belongs here. Don't worry, the past isn't going to repeat itself. I won't let it."

Val sighed. "I'd like to believe that, Miss Ellie, but I think it's already beginning to happen."

Miss Ellie shook her head in wonder. "Valene, I think you're imagining things. I understand why you'd be wary, but J.R. and Jock have really made a wonderful effort so far, and that's going to make all the difference. More tea?" she offered, but Val declined. It was no use. Whatever was happening, Miss Ellie wasn't going to see it until it blew up in front of her face.

As Val made her way out of the sliding glass door,

she ran into Bobby, nearly knocking him over.

"What's going on, Val? You look upset," he asked her.

"Oh, I don't know what's going on—I can't make up my mind whether to cut and run or stay and fight."

Bobby was confused. As far as he could see, things had been going more smoothly than anyone could have ever expected. Yet here was Valene, acting as if there were a war on. "Fight with who?" he wanted to know. But she couldn't tell him—she didn't know herself. Instead of answering, she drew him into the dining room where they could talk more privately.

Sitting herself on the edge of the table, she asked, "Bobby—what's J.R. up to?"

Bobby shrugged. "Nothing, as far as I can tell. He just gave Gary some stuff to read through about this business, is all. Why? What's got you so worried?"

Val leaned into him and spoke in a whisper. They were clearly alone, yet she felt she needed to be careful. "You were only a kid—you don't remember—this kind of thing chews Gary up and spits him out. Oh, I know what you're thinking— he can take care of himself; he wants to work. Sure he wants to work, but Bobby, I tell you, that man is not cut out for this stuff — he's no businessman! J.R. is doing it to get rid of him, I just know it!"

Bobby couldn't believe what he was hearing. He might have been a kid last time, but he'd been there today! Gary was settled now, a grown man! And J.R. may have pushed a bit too hard, but he couldn't believe his brother would be so contriving as to engineer such a convoluted way to get rid of somebody. It was too devious to be human, even for J.R.

He felt sure Valene was exaggerating, letting her fears get the better of her. Nevertheless, to soothe her he said, "Listen, I'll tell Gary to take it slow. If this thing doesn't work out, we can always think of something else. Just don't worry so much—you'll see—it'll all work out fine."

Val thanked him and got up to go. Somehow, in spite of everyone's assurances, she felt surer than ever that it was not paradise that was approaching, but disaster.

Out on the patio, Sue Ellen sat in a deck chair crocheting. She worked the needles as if they were stilettos, all her suppressed anger finding expression in the click of needle against needle, as if she were sticking them through the bodies of her enemies. Next to her, J.R. lay sprawled on a chaise reading a newspaper. He held the paper out in front of his face, both to shield him from the sun and to hide from his wife's view. He was as content as she was upset, and he didn't want to flaunt that contentment in front of her and arouse her anger further.

"My," she said off-handedly, "haven't you been nice and brotherly to that boy since he got here! Apologizing to him, and then giving him a whole business to look after! That's quite a welcome. Aren't we charitable lately?"

J.R. ignored her remark. "Says here there's a tax revolt in California, gonna spread all through the country. Did you say something to me, Sue Ellen?"

Sue Ellen pouted and threw down her work.

"Don't you ever listen to a word I say?" she spat out.

"Why, darlin', I hang on your every word, you know that," drawled J.R., the essence of submissive charm.

"I was talking about Gary," she reminded him.

"Is that what's bothering you, honey? Don't give it another thought. Old Gary is on board a sinking ship, and he's hard at work trying to bail it out with an eye-dropper."

J.R. caught sight of Bobby and cut short what he was saying to greet his brother. But Bobby, in spite of himself, had been affected by Val's fears and felt he had to sound J.R. out just to be sure there was nothing sinister going on. "Any idea where Gary is?" he asked.

"I think," said J.R., "that he's still hard at work, nose to the grindstone."

Bobby sat down next to his brother. "Maybe we should find something else for him to get into, J.R.," he offered.

J.R. sat up, a look of incredulity on his face. "Hey, Bob, this isn't a department store. I don't have a large selection of businesses to choose from."

"Maybe he shouldn't be in any business at all yet. There's no rush, is there?"

J.R. draped a hand over his brother's shoulder as if he were a slow child who needed every last little thing explained to him. "Bobby, that business is a gold mine! And any moron can run it successfully. Gary'll get it started; Mama'll be on cloud nine, and we'll all ride off into the sunset and live happily ever after, believe me."

Bobby couldn't argue with J.R.'s logic. Besides,

he really had no idea what Gary was or was not capable of. He'd only been a child. He hoped J.R. was right, because he'd come to love his new brother in just a short time. "I hope you're right, J.R.—I want my brother to hang around," he said, a note of warning in his voice.

Sue Ellen looked up and said to no one in particular, "Of course—the more the merrier!"

Bobby ignored Sue Ellen. But to J.R., he felt he had to add one more word of direct warning to head off any possible danger: "Don't try anything funny, J.R.," he said.

J.R. had had enough. He threw down his newspaper and, with all the fury he could manufacture, he retorted, "What the hell do you mean by that? I've done everything to keep that boy here!"

"Good," said Bobby, looking him right in the eye, "and when he decides to stay, I'll thank you for it. But you'd better mean what you say."

J.R. smiled at him, a crooked little smile, and said softly, "I always mean what I say, little brother. One way or another."

Before Bobby could register what J.R. had said, Pam's car pulled up in the driveway. It was clear to him at once that she was devastated, on the verge of tears. He ran to put his arm around her, but she pulled away and ran into the house. He followed her inside. They both stopped as they saw Jock coming down the stairs. "How's Digger?" he asked.

Flashing her eyes in fury at him, Pam answered, "Just wonderful, thank you!"

Jock ignored her tone and asked where he was. "He's at Maggie's, Daddy," Bobby explained.

"Well, let me know if there's any way I can help," said Jock, continuing downstairs.

"You've helped more than enough already!" Pam hissed.

Jock turned, not angrily but firmly, and said, "I don't think punishing me is going to make you feel any better, but if it does, I don't mind."

Stung, but still furious, Pam continued up the stairs. Bobby looked after her, hurting for her.

Chapter Twelve

After his unpleasant encounter with Pamela, Jock strode out onto the porch and carefully placed his large frame in his favorite rocker. It bothered him greatly that Pam was angry at him. He felt, deep in his heart, that whatever had happened between him and Digger Barnes was in the distant past and ought to be forgotten. He could not help the fact that Digger had become a hopeless drunk. Whatever Digger might tell himself and the world, a man's destiny is in his own hands, and if he winds up in the gutter he's got nobody to blame but himself.

So thought Jock Ewing as he sat on the porch of his mansion watching the sun sink lower over the vast ranch that was his home. He felt for Digger, but he wasn't going to give in to him no matter how angry his daughter-in-law got with him. Life had been good to Jock, and he felt it his duty to enjoy it as much as possible and not be dragged down with the failures of the world just because they'd been unlucky. Maybe he had played fast and loose with Digger a couple of times, but he couldn't be blamed for the way things had turned out.

The sound of screeching brakes and burning tire rubber brought him back to earth. From the entrance to the ranch an old Chevy came careening toward him, weaving its way half on the road, half on the lawn. Jock stood up, furious. Alerted by the commotion, the rest of the family poured out the back door, one by one, to see what was happening.

The car finally slammed into a wooden post near the porch and came to a halt. Out of the driver's side stumbled Digger Barnes, drunk as could be, carrying the bag of things Pam had brought for him. Pam, standing on the porch, was horrified.

"Barnes!" bellowed Jock Ewing. "What the hell's gotten into you?"

Digger reached into the bag and began flinging the books and magazines toward Pam. "I don't want charity from the dirty rich!" he screamed in a frenzy, foaming at the corners of the mouth. "Give this stuff to the crippled and the maimed— to the decrepit and the diseased—I don't want your charity, you condescending sons of bitches— I came here to discuss business!"

The whole family stood frozen in place, stunned by the obvious insanity of the pitiable man staggering in front of them. Jock strode forward and faced Digger head on. "All right, you've returned the gifts, now get out of here!"

"Yeah, I've returned them," Digger retorted, "but I'm not leaving till I've got what belongs to me by right!"

"And what," sneered Jock, "might that be *this* time?"

"You can't argue with this one, Ewing. You took all my oil wells, you took my girl..." he looked at Miss Ellie standing mortified on the porch, "and I never got a nickel for any of it! Well, the statute of limitations has run out on all that, I guess, although you'll get yours in the next life, if there is one..."

Jock was growing impatient listening to all this drivel. "Get to the point, Barnes—I'm tired of listening to all this bushwa!"

A drunken smile crossed Digger's lips. "I want money," he said, "money for the only thing I had left to take." He glanced meaningfully at Pam and smiled smugly. "She used to be mine, just like everything else you've got." He looked again at Jock to test the effect of his words.

Jock was disgusted. No matter what had happened to him, Digger ought to have kept a little dignity; instead he seemed to revel in the depths to which he had sunk.

"How much?" he asked.

Digger put his hands in his pockets and swayed back and forth. "Twenty thousand," he replied.

Jock shook his head in disbelief. He knew damned well he wasn't going to get anything of the kind, yet he had deliberately asked for the outrageous sum, knowing he would be turned down flat. Instead of turning his back on the pitiful waste of a man in front of him, Jock took out a wad of bills and peeled off a hundred dollars. He wanted to throw them on the ground and make Digger dive for them, but in deference to Pamela, he handed them to him.

"I'll take it!" said Digger, tipping his hat to everyone. "Beggars can't be choosers. Ladies... Gentlemen..." And with a bow, he got back into the car and drove off, as recklessly as he had come.

Pam hadn't breathed for over a minute. The whole scene had cut through her like a knife, bringing home to her in the most painful way possible her father's degradation and Jock Ewing's self-satisfied cynicism. Turning to Gary, who stood rooted to the porch next to her, she hissed, "There! Aren't you glad you're back in the bosom of your wonderful family?" Spinning on her heels, she marched back into the house, leaving behind her a very shaken Gary.

As Bobby rushed to their bedroom, he found Pam already heading for the shower. With all the energy she could muster, she tried to hold her rage tightly inside. Her rage was her own, and nobody, not even Bobby, was going to take that away from her.

"Honey," Bobby began, trying his best to calm her down. But Pam wasn't having any.

"I'm fine!" she lied, continuing to prepare for her shower.

"What?" Bobby was incredulous. She had never acted like this with him before. They had always been open and truthful with each other—it was the cornerstone of their relationship—and now she was keeping her inner heart out of his reach.

"I'm just fine. You know why? Because I'm past caring—I don't give a damn!" She flung a towel on the bed as if it were her worst enemy and she meant to destroy it.

"Oh, come on, don't try to kid me..." Bobby said, again reaching for her. But again she spun out of his grasp.

"It's true," she repeated. "I don't care in the least. Why should I? Why should I care about a drunken old fool who smells like a sewer and contaminates everyone he comes close to! The sooner I wash him out of my system the better!" And with that, she turned and went into the bathroom. Bobby followed her, sitting down on the edge of the tub.

"Why don't you just talk to me?" he offered.

She shook him off again. "Because I don't need to talk to anyone. I can handle it just fine on my own, thank you." But both of them could hear the stifled scream that made a lump in her throat and almost prevented her from speaking.

Wanting to bring the subject to a close, she asked him how Gary was making out. Bobby, sensing her purpose, let the conversation turn to his brother.

"I think he was okay until just now—that little scene shook him up rather badly, from what I could see." Pam stopped for a moment, remembering her conversation with Gary in Las Vegas when she had agreed to serve as a crutch for him if he needed her. How could she help him, or anybody else, in the state she was in? And how was he going to get by without her in this awful place? She resolved to speak with him later, to try to sound him out. There was no way she would ever be happy living here, she thought in her anger, but the least she could do was try to help someone else.

Bobby watched his wife closely, more worried

than he had ever been about the future of their relationship. Something had to give, somewhere; he could see that. He only hoped it wouldn't be their marriage.

Dinner had come and gone, and night had fallen over Southfork. In the little study off the main hallway, Gary sat alone going over the pamphlets J.R. had piled in front of him. With every passing minute, Gary felt himself sinking deeper and deeper, his hopes retreating further and further out of his grasp. Why was he so incompetent? Why was he such an idiot about business? Was there no place for him here? No place at all? Determinedly he dove back into the papers, but he could feel his determination was beginning to wear thin. A sense of dread and despair pumped through his body with every pulsing heartbeat, and his mood was growing as black as the Southfork night.

The knock on the door came like a welcome relief. Pamela poked her head in, smiling apologetically. "Mind if we talk for a minute?"

"Not at all—come on in," Gary said gratefully. He wanted desperately to share his feelings with someone, someone who wasn't depending on him the way everybody else seemed to be doing. Yet, he felt guilty for every second he took away from the studies he felt he should be devoting himself to.

"I wanted to apologize for yelling at you this afternoon. It was awful of me."

Gary patted her head affectionately. "It must have been terrible for you," he said sympathetically.

"What a drama, huh?" she laughed, embarrassed

and ashamed for her father's behavior.

"Yeah," he agreed, the troubled look spreading over his face, "this place is a million laughs, isn't it?"

Pam shrugged. "I suppose so, if you look at it that way...are you all right?"

Gary sighed deeply. "Oh, sure. See this report? I've read through the first page of it twenty-two times."

"It sounds complicated," Pam ventured.

Gary shook his head. "It's as simple as can be. It's not the pamphlet, it's me. I can't start reading without my mind wandering every five seconds... I start thinking of...oh, just anything! What color the wallpaper in my room is, whether my new jeans are at the laundry—my concentration's shot to hell!" He threw the pamphlet on the table in frustration.

"Hey, take it easy, Gary!" she warned him, "It's natural to be nervous. Don't worry, you'll get over it, you'll see."

Gary nodded, unconvinced. "I guess so..."

As if on cue, to help ease the discomfort between two uncomfortable people, Miss Ellie peeked through the door and asked if she could come in with some milk and cookies. Pam and Gary looked at each other and almost burst out laughing. It was such a relief to see someone so untroubled, so immune to the darker currents flowing around the house. Somehow, it made them both feel better, at least for the moment.

"How are you doing, Pam? Any better?" she asked gently.

"Yes, Miss Ellie, thank you," said Pam. She thought for a moment of her father and Miss Ellie.

They had been sweethearts once, long ago, before she had married Jock...Pam shook her head. The idea of her father with this woman was as incongruous as her presence in this house of turmoil. Somehow, Miss Ellie belonged on a southern plantation wearing hoop skirts, dancing the Virginia Reel, fanning herself flirtatiously. What a lot of trouble she'd had to put up with! Pam shook her head in admiration. If only she could learn to deal with trouble as well!

Miss Ellie set the tray down on the desk in front of Gary. "Gary," she said, concerned, "don't forget to go to sleep at a reasonable hour..."

"I won't, Mama," he said absently.

Passing by the open door, Lucy looked in and saw the three of them together. Figuring that her father must be taking a well-deserved break, she joined them. Kissing her father on the forehead and hugging him tightly, she joked, "You must be an expert at this business by this time!"

Miss Ellie caught the worry in Gary's eyes. "Maybe you ought to stop for the night, Gary," she suggested. "After all, you don't have to learn it all at once, do you?"

Gary laughed mirthlessly. "I was hoping to learn at least *one* thing, anyway," he quipped.

His tone worried Pam. She saw now that he was in serious trouble. Perhaps the best thing was to leave him alone to use his own resources as best he could. She excused herself, saying she was tired and was going to bed, and urged Gary one last time to take it easy on himself. Taking the hint from Pam, Miss Ellie turned to Lucy and gently suggested that they leave Gary to his studies.

Knowing her grandmother was right, she

leaned over to kiss her father goodnight. As Gary turned back to the desk, his elbow caught the edge of the tray, spilling the glass of milk. Before he could react, the milk began to penetrate the papers on the desk. Gary stared at the disaster helplessly while, around him, the three women rushed to clean up the mess before too much damage was done. Lucy ran to get some napkins, while Pam took some papers that were not yet ruined from the desk. Grabbing his handkerchief from his back pocket, Gary began wiping up the spill, but he was so nervous and overwrought that he wound up knocking over the glass a second time, spilling the rest of the milk all over the desk, doing much more damage than even the first spill. Gary stared stupidly at the advancing flood, as if he were staring at his life's blood flowing away, washing away all his hopes and dreams with it. What an absurd way to go, was all he could think. He stood frozen, watching the disaster, as the three women did what they could to minimize the already considerable damage.

"I'm sorry...I'm so sorry..." he kept repeating over and over again. He couldn't help feeling he had somehow willed this to happen by his inner reluctance to succeed. What made it even worse was that the women were embarrassed for him and kept trying to reassure him that everything was okay. Finally, he felt himself exploding and heard himself scream at the top of his lungs, "Will you leave me alone! It's just a stupid glass of milk!"

His own paralysis in the face of disaster, coupled with the efficiency of the women in dealing with it, overcame him, and he ran from the room in tears, a complete wreck of a man.

Lucy wanted to follow, but Miss Ellie stopped her. She knew he needed to be alone; still, she was shocked at the depth of his reaction. Had she been blind to his torment all this time? Had she completely missed what was going on? Most of all, the question that haunted her was, am I too late? Have I lost him again?

Chapter Thirteen

It was late at night and the house was eerily quiet. Night lights strategically placed here and there threw half-shadows on the walls, silhouetting the furniture, making the chairs seem like looming ghosts standing very still.

Down the stairs crept a moving shadow, tiptoeing so as not to waken anyone else. The shadow advanced away from the kitchen into the family room and over to the liquor cabinet. Gary Ewing wondered if his mother was waiting for him in the kitchen with another glass of milk. How ironic that that milk should have been the catalyst of his destruction!

He reached for a bottle and a glass. He could tell from long experience with the shapes of bottles, that it was bourbon. It didn't matter; it could have been rye, or scotch, or gin. Two days at home with the Ewings had driven him to the breaking point. For years, he had stayed sober, and now he was on the edge of throwing it all away. His hands, steady for the first time in two days, poured a full glass. He held it up in front of him in the dim light.

Behind him, and unseen by him, another shadow crossed the doorway of the living room. In silhouette, Valene watched the only man she had ever really loved battling for his life. She ached for him and wanted desperately to go to him. But somehow, she couldn't. Something inside her held her back. Unable to watch his destruction, she turned around silently and tiptoed back upstairs.

Unaware that he had been observed, Gary continued to hold the glass in front of his lips for what seemed an eternity. Finally, the war inside of him was decided. He poured the sweet poison down the drain of the bar sink, put the bottle back in its place, turned, and left the room, a shattered man, but still a man.

The sun rose blood red on another day, already as hot as midday should be. Even the birds seemed too tired to chirp. The roosters did not even try. The day was going to be oppressive, no doubt about it.

The front door of the mansion opened slowly and Gary Ewing stood in the doorway, his suitcase in his hand. He took a last, long look around him, trying to impress every detail on his brain. Who could say when, if ever, he would see this place again? Then, knowing he could not delay without having to say goodbye, he started down the path.

Watching him retreat from an upstairs window was J.R. Ewing, his face concealing all emotions that might have been roiling under the surface, content to let the current take events downstream. His brother was going away; dealing with Valene would be a simple matter once he was gone.

J.R.'s gaze was distracted by the front door opening again. It was Valene, dressed only in her nightgown, her blonde hair cascading over her shoulders. "Gary!" she shouted after him.

But Gary, if he heard her, just kept walking steadily, determinedly. Without bothering to shout after him again, worried anyway that her shouts might rouse the household, she ran after him and caught up to him about halfway to the main gate of the ranch. Again she called his name, a plea in her voice. He stopped but didn't turn around. Resolutely she stepped around in front of him so she could see his face. It was streaked with tears, and his eyes had a faraway look in them as if they were focused on something terribly important and just as distant.

She had to make him talk to her, otherwise there was no way she could get him to stay. She didn't want him to think she'd been spying on him, but she felt it was the only way to make him focus on her. "I saw you last night—pouring that drink...did you...?"

His eyes came back and now looked straight at her. "Did I take the drink? Is that what you're asking? No, I didn't, Val. But I almost did. It was everything I could do to resist it. I've only been here a couple of days, and already I've lost years of progress. I knew right then that I had to leave this place if I was going to stay sane and sober. It's the only way, believe me."

Val took him by the shoulders. "If you have to leave, at least don't leave like this—"

"I don't know any other way, Val," he replied.

"But you can't do this to Lucy! You can't leave without telling her, without explaining! It's her whole life, you and me being back with her! Think what it'll do to her—you can't just go like this, Gary, you can't!"

Gary's face bore a look of infinite weight, the weight of great sadness. "Better she should hate me for running out on her than hate her whole family for driving me away—she's got a life here, a home, school, friends, stability—with me she'd have nothing. I can't do that to her, Val. I love her too much."

Val felt her heart in her throat. She had felt the same way when she'd given Lucy up to J.R.'s thugs all those years ago. But now she felt she knew better. "She needs her real family, Gary—that's more important to her than all those other things, believe me."

But Gary just shook his head and smiled sadly. His experience of the past two days had proved to him that he couldn't take care of anyone. He had all he could do just to take care of himself!

Val knew she had to try another tack. "Gary, if you go, think what will happen to me! How long do you think I'll last around here without you?"

Gary winced. He couldn't bear to think of it, but there was nothing he could do. "I've got to go, Val—it's the only way," he said.

It was so ironic, thought Val. She had known he was going because she had come to his room. She had finally come to him and he had been gone! Desperately, she told him about it, hoping against hope that it would make him stay.

"Did you come to me for Auld Lang Syne?" he asked.

"For the future, Gary—for New Time's sake. Please, honey—just come back for a little while. I want you so bad..." And she kissed him full and long on the lips. He responded with all the passion of his agony and his loss and his loneliness, and when the kiss was over, he sighed deeply.

"I have to go. Right now, or I'm never going to make it. You know, at first I thought it was me...that I was just no good. It took me sixteen years of struggle, and two days here with you and with Lucy...and with them...and I realize now, for the first time, that that's not it at all! I'm fine. I really am all right. As a person, you know? It's just that I don't belong here. With them, I'm not myself, at least not the way I want to be. There's nothing wrong with me that wouldn't be fixed by being somewhere else. I'm gonna be all right, Val, don't you worry," he added, seeing her concern and her agony at losing him. He kissed her again, long and slowly, and as tenderly as any kiss can be given. When he finished he said, "I'll let you know where I am, soon as I get settled someplace, and maybe you can come join me."

She looked at him, feeling it might be for the last time. How would he be able to get in touch with her if she had to run for her life? But she wanted to believe his words, wanted so much to believe this man.

"I love you, Gary. I've loved you since the day I met you, and I always will. You're my knight in shining armor, honey, no matter how tattered you think you are." The tears were coming faster now, falling from her chin onto her nightgown, staining it with sadness. Gary kissed her once on the cheek and then, turning away, he slowly walked out into the future, leaving behind everything he had been, everyone he had ever loved.

It was several minutes before Valene turned around and started walking back to the house. The sun was in her eyes as she walked, and so it was not until she was less than twenty yards from the porch that she noticed that there was someone sitting in Jock's favorite rocking chair staring at her intently. It was J.R. Had he seen the whole thing? Val knew in her heart that he had, just as he had seen everything almost before it happened. She wondered if J.R. really was in league with the devil, or if, perhaps, he was the devil himself.

"Why, Valene," he said solicitously, when she reached the foot of the steps, "you'll catch cold out here in that skimpy little nighty."

J.R. never ceased to catch her off guard with the depth of his evil. "I get sick anywhere near you," she said, bitterly.

"Well then, you'd be better off far away from me, don't you agree?" he smiled cheerfully.

She walked up the stairs and stood over him. "You played us like violins, J.R." she said wonderingly.

"Why, thank you Valene. I'd have to agree with you there, although I don't like to toot my own horn." One side of his mouth curled up into a wicked grin.

"What are my chances around here now?" she asked, knowing the answer.

"I'd say 'slim' just left, if you catch my drift," he quipped.

"Have I got any options?" she asked, trying in

her own defense to be as calculating as she could.

"Why, yes. I'm glad you asked me that question, Valene, because it shows you're intelligent enough to keep your head about you when the chips are down. You'll do all right for yourself once you get out of Texas, away from all the memories and the stresses of family life."

"What are you saying?" Val said impatiently, doing all she could to keep from attacking him.

"I'll give you a five thousand dollar head start, and an escort to the state line."

Val bowed her head. All the fight had drained out of her. "Why did you do this? That's what I want to know, J.R. You took away a girl's father and mother; you murdered her dreams, and you lost yourself a brother, all at the same time, and for what? Just tell me that!"

"I have enough brothers in my hair without Gary around," J.R. said ominously.

"He wouldn't have been any threat to you!" Val was incredulous. That J.R. should have been threatened by Gary was unbelievable! "He wasn't after your position, your power. All he would have done was give you his love, and you could have used that—you sure could have used that."

J.R.'s face clouded over in anger. "Go get your stuff together, and put some clothes on. I'll call the escort service," he murmured, "and I'll write you out that check, too."

Val exploded. "I don't want your goddamn blood money!" she hissed. "You've taken everything I've ever had, or loved, or cared a damn about. You've ruined my life, J.R., but one thing you can't do is buy me. Take your Ewing money and stuff it!" She went inside, slamming the door behind her.

***

J.R. went to the breakfast table and helped himself to some coffee from the hot pot Raoul had provided. He sat back in his chair, vastly contented with himself. He stared at the blue flame of the sterno under the coffee pot, and gave himself over to reflection. Things had gone beautifully, and he had managed it without ever showing his hand, without losing one ounce of his daddy's good graces. Nobody could accuse him of anything, and yet he had done everything! He laughed softly to himself. Then he stopped laughing abruptly.

He had been staring at the far end of the table where Lucy always sat at mealtimes, and his eye had been drawn to a fleck of white protruding from under her plate. Putting down his coffee, he sidled over to it, knowing even before he got a good look at it what the piece of paper was. Tearing open the envelope, he read the note inside from start to finish. He had to give Valene credit. Even in the letter, she didn't mention him, didn't refer to his subtle machinations. Trashy as she was, he had to admit that Valene had a certain amount of natural class underneath it all. The note was mostly about how they would all be together again soon, far away from Southfork, and not to give up hope, or think badly of either of them for leaving so suddenly.

J.R. went over to the coffeepot, and sliding the letter underneath it, he watched as the blue flames of the sterno fire consumed it, little by little, until there was nothing left. Then he took the five thousand dollar check out of his pocket, the check that would never be cashed. He fed it, too, to the flame, sending it after the note like a doomed messenger. Smiling the smile of the victor, J.R. sat back down and finished his coffee. It tasted especially good this morning. He made a note to himself to compliment Raoul about it. He couldn't remember when he'd felt better.

Chapter Fourteen

It was the proverbial morning after the night before, except that there had been no party, no drunkenness, no revelry. Nevertheless, thought Raoul as he served them all their breakfast outside on the patio, the group at the table had the aspect of a funeral, their stunned expressions and listless movements the clearest sign of the shock they had all sustained. Even J.R. looked upset, Raoul noticed, in spite of the fact that he had seemed cheerful earlier that morning when he had had his coffee alone in the dining room. Perhaps, thought Raoul, he had not known then about the disappearances of Mister Gary and Miss Valene. Or perhaps... Raoul had been with the Ewings a long time; long enough to know that J.R.'s feelings could be well disguised when he wanted them to be. Raoul had also been around long enough to know when to keep quiet. This was one of those times.

There were four family members at the table:

Jock and Miss Ellie, J.R. and Sue Ellen. But everyone had been awake for a long time, and everyone knew that Gary and Val had gone. Miss Ellie was devastated. She just could not understand what had happened. Everything had seemed to be going so well—her life had finally seemed to be coming together in a way it hadn't done for years, and then—she just couldn't understand how things changed so fast without her even being aware that anything was amiss. It didn't make any sense to her. Things just didn't happen that way! J.R. tried in vain to soothe her.

To Jock Ewing, the whole affair was disconcerting in a much different way. He had really thought Gary had grown up, settled down and matured. What he couldn't understand was how his son could have seemed so right on his feet when the truth was that he was just the same confused, weak adolescent he had always been. Jock was disappointed, deeply disappointed, and angry for what Gary had done to Miss Ellie. Look at her, he thought! She's about to bust out crying. If I had that boy here, and a good willow switch, I'd give him a good lick for every tear his mother ever shed over him.

Bobby and Pam emerged on the patio, Lucy between them in one of her spitfire moods. She was furious at her father, and no matter how much Pam and Bobby tried to calm her, tried to make her understand what her father must have been going through, she wasn't having any of it. She yanked her arms from their grasp and walked on ahead of them. She didn't love her father. She hated him. He wasn't worthy of her love, or even of her pity. She thought with scorn of the way he had panicked over a little spilled milk. And this was the man she had worshiped in her dreams all her life! She felt suddenly as if she were fifty years old, wise with bitter experience. Pam and Bobby urged her not to jump to conclusions. Both of them felt, although they could not say why, that there was more to it than met the eye. They felt close enough to Gary, and sure enough of his regard for them, to know that he would have shared his reasons for leaving with them if he could have. Bobby looked at J.R. as they arrived at the table. His brother's face reflected complete lack of knowledge about what had gone on. But Bobby wondered—Valene had been so sure he was after them...

"J.R.," he said, quietly, but with an undertone of menace in his voice, "we need to talk. I think you know more about this than you're saying, and I've got a lot of questions I want answers to."

But J.R. brushed him off: "Bobby, I'm surprised at you. Can't you see Mama and Lucy are upset? This is not the time for raking up the mud, little brother. Now eat your breakfast, and leave us all in peace."

Sue Ellen ate her breakfast with gusto. "I don't know how you expect anyone to eat, what with all the commotion!" she said to her husband. She felt so pleased with him, and with the way things had turned out, that she could barely conceal her glee.

Lucy sat down at the table, more to get out of Bobby and Pam's friendly clutches than to eat any food. "If he ever decides to come back to Southfork, somebody please tell me first—so I can arrange not to be here!"

Pam was shocked. Lucy was being childish and unfair, and she felt she had to say something.

"Lucy, he's your father! Don't talk like that."

Lucy looked daggers at her. "You're a fine one to talk. You're the last person in the world to give advice on father-daughter relationships!"

Pam's cheeks stung as if they'd been slapped.

"Lucy," said Bobby sternly, "that's enough."

But it was too late. Pam stood up and excused herself from the table. As she went, she turned to Lucy. "Life isn't fair, Lucy. That doesn't mean you stop trying to straighten things out." And with that, she ran to her car, revved the engine, and sped away.

At the table, no one said a word. Everybody seemed to be running away today. Lucy asked J.R. where her mother had gone, and J.R., somewhat tentatively, replied that he thought she'd said she was going to look for Gary. Lucy breathed a little easier. "At least I know *she'll* still be here for me," she said, comforting herself.

Bobby looked over at J.R. out of the corner of his eye. J.R. returned his glance meaningfully. What did he know that he wasn't telling, Bobby wondered. He had to find out, but not here. Later, when they were alone, he would get some answers.

Ellie excused herself from the table, too, and walked out toward the range. Jock got up to follow her. He caught up to her after about fifty yards and asked if he could walk with her, but Ellie told him she needed to be alone. Her whole life had fallen apart, and she had to figure out how and why it had happened. Jock stared after her. He told himself he'd never let himself get his hopes up that high again. People don't change, he said to himself.

***

Digger Barnes woke with a start from his drunken stupor, and looked up as the door of his room swung open. Pamela stood there, breathing hard, having run all the way from the car.

"Hey!" he cried, "didn't I forbid you—"

"Never mind that!" she interrupted him. "I'm not having any more of that nonsense. You're a lush, and you behave like a moron—you make me ashamed to be your daughter."

"I didn't go and marry one of them!" the old man retorted.

"Well, I did, and I'm very glad I did, too!" she shouted back. "Boby Ewing is a fine man, and I've never had to be ashamed of *him*! I have to put up with the rest of his family—so does he, for that matter. I put up with them, just like I put up with you."

Digger got up from the bed and faced his daughter. "Who asked you to put up with me? If you don't like it get out! It's what I told you to do in the first place!"

"I can't get out!" She was screaming now, with all the fury and frustration she had kept inside her for so long. "You're my father, whatever I think of you, and I can't change that. Next to Jock Ewing, you're the most awful man I know, but I love you, and I'm never going to get out of your life! Ever! Do you hear me?"

Digger stood frozen to the spot, shocked into immobility by his daughter's unanticipated fury. "Get out," he whispered weakly.

Pam smiled the smile of triumph. "I'll be back. Again and again."

"You're wasting your time," he rasped.

"It's my time to waste. And you'll see me, sooner or later." Turning from him, she walked out, closing the door behind her.

For a moment, he stood there immobile. Then he called out, "Pamela!" The door opened immediately—she'd been just on the other side of it. He went to the bedside table and picked up the hundred dollars Jock had given him. Holding them out to her, he said, "Take these back to him."

Pam shook her head. "Are you crazy? He owes you everything he's got. The least you can do is keep it." Coming up to the stubborn old man who was her father, and whom she loved with all her heart, she kissed him on the cheek and left. Standing, holding the bills in front of him and smiling, Digger Barnes looked at the spot where she had stood. He'd done something right in his life after all. He'd raised her.

It was late afternoon. Valene had not returned, and Lucy had begun to grow anxious. She paced back and forth on the porch, staring out in the distance hoping to catch a glimpse of her mother. Inside, as the family sat together in the living room, the feelings everyone had kept to themselves all day began to percolate to the surface. Jock Ewing was steaming, having worked himself into a quiet fury.

"If I ever see that boy again, I'm gonna take him apart for what he's done to his mama." Miss Ellie, tired and depressed, had gone straight up to bed after their early dinner. It had been all she could do to get through the meal without breaking down.

J.R. was cool and cynical. "I always knew Gary was like that. I don't know why we let ourselves believe any different."

Pam looked up. She was sure J.R. had had something to do with Gary's disappearance, and she wasn't about to let him sully Gary in his absence.

"How do you mean?" she challenged him. "Like what?"

Sue Ellen looked up from her crossword. "You know perfectly well what he means, Pamela dear."

Pam was full of fight, fresh from the day's triumph with her father, and she wasn't going to let this one go by. "I do know what he means, and I resent the implication that Gary was somehow bad because he wasn't like you all think a Ewing ought to be. He was a good man, and he still is, and if he ran away from this place, I'm sure he had good reason!"

Sue Ellen threw down her book. "Really, Pamela! Lower your voice! You'll disturb Miss Ellie!" she admonished her.

Bobby now entered the fray in defense of his wife. "I'd like to know what his reasons were, as a matter of fact. I've been waiting to hear them all day, J.R."

J.R. looked at his father as if to say, 'You and I understand all this, don't we, Daddy?' and then, turning to Bobby, he said, "Gary left because he has no character. It's as simple as that."

"You mean," Bobby retorted, "that he hasn't got the kind of character you've got. He's a man with sensitivity—a creative man, who likes animals, and plants, and painting, and books—not a man you'd have much respect for, I'm sure. But I happen to like Gary Ewing!''

Hearing the raised voices from the living room, Miss Ellie had come downstairs. She joined her husband on the sofa. Her face wore an expression of deep concern and grief, but she said nothing, did nothing to stem the overflow of pent-up emotions that was occurring.

J.R. continued to defend his position. "Gary's a weakling, Bob. He just couldn't hack it.''

"Oh come on, J.R.!'' his brother shot back at him. "To you, anyone's weak who hasn't got it in him to stab someone in the back to get ahead!''

J.R. sat back looking almost pleased to have recovered the moral high ground. "I forgive you for that, Bobby. You're upset, and I'll assume that you don't know what you're saying.''

But Bobby was not ready to let the matter go. To him a colossal injustice had been done, and he felt it was somehow up to him to bring it all out into the open.

"I don't understand the way you think J.R.,'' he said. "Why is a man weak just because he's sensitive? Is it necessary to be ruthless in order for a man to meet with your approval?''

J.R. shrugged. "Ruthlessness is the way of the world, Bob. You've got to protect what's yours and go after what isn't yours but ought to be. If a man's not ruthless, pretty soon he won't have anything left to call his own. It's a simple fact of life.''

Bobby wanted to get back to Gary and away from grandiose talk about the way of the world. "I like my brother, Gary. I've never met somebody with his kind of outlook, his perspective, his humor..."

"His way of walking out on his family and his daughter? For the *second* time? You like that, too?" J.R. finished his sentence for him.

Bobby had had all he could take. He burst out with what was really on his mind and had been all along. "J.R.," he said, "I don't believe Gary left willingly. I believe you forced him out."

Audible gasps could be heard all around the room. Miss Ellie was the first to speak. "Bobby! That's not fair to your brother!"

Jock agreed. "Bob, now go easy on J.R. We all did our darnedest to make Gary feel at home. It just didn't work."

Bobby went over to his father. "Daddy," he said urgently, "you and Mama and me, we all did our best. But J.R.—he knew Gary couldn't deal with business. That's why he laid those papers on him—and he just kept pushing and pushing until he'd pushed Gary away from here for good!"

J.R. shot up from his chair. "You take back that vicious accusation, brother!" he demanded.

But Bobby wasn't finished. "J.R., I wanted Gary to make it here. He's a good human being, and I learned a lot from him in just a little time. Somehow...I'm still not sure how, you managed to get it into his head that he wasn't good enough to be a Ewing. I didn't know how to stop you, and for that I'm ashamed of myself. I'm proud to be related to Gary, but J.R., you make me ashamed to be a Ewing."

Bobby sat down. In the room there was only stunned silence. Pam took her husband's hands and looked into his eyes proudly and lovingly. The argument was over, its energy spent. Now from the hall, they could hear Lucy on the phone with Pete, telling him to call her back if Val showed up at the diner.

"I just talked to Pete," she said mournfully as she returned to the living room. "He says she hasn't been there. I just don't understand it. Oh, well, maybe she found Daddy. Maybe she's trying to convince him to come back. That's probably why she hasn't called or..."

J.R. spoke up, the shadow of doom in his voice. "Don't get your hopes up, Lucy." Lucy looked at him, puzzled. "When I said she'd gone after him, I was just trying to spare your feelings..." He trailed off.

Jock looked at him, wide-eyed. "J.R., if there's something you're not telling us, spit it out."

J.R. shook his head. "I don't think that would be a good idea, Daddy." He was going to make them think they were prying it out of him. It was all part of the plan. He'd been saving it for the right moment, and the right moment was now.

Sue Ellen urged him on, saying it was preferable for Lucy to face the truth head on, than for her to go on nursing fantasies for the rest of her life. Ellie began to protest, feeling perhaps if the truth was so awful it were better left unsaid. Lucy stood up and demanded to know what J.R. was hiding from her.

J.R. walked over to the desk and opened a drawer. From it he took out a large, black checkbook. Bringing it over to Lucy, he opened it in front of her and pointed to one of the stubs. Lucy's voice choked as she read, her eyes not willing to believe what they were seeing. The check had been made out to her mother for five thousand dollars, and J.R. had signed it. "She asked me for money in exchange for leaving," lied J.R. "That was her price." The check would never be cashed, but Lucy would never know that. The evidence in front of her eyes was all the evidence she would need to condemn her mother.

"Honey," said J.R., a note of sympathy oozing from his voice, "I know the truth is hard to take sometimes, but—" Before he could go on, Lucy spit right in his face and ran sobbing from the room.

J.R. took his handkerchief from his pocket and wiped his face. It was a small price to pay for what he had achieved. In ancient Greece the messenger who brought the bad news was killed. He had only been spat upon. Everyone in the room was silent. Everyone knew. In their own, clouded, oblique way, they knew something fishy had happened. But they also knew there was nothing to be done about it now. They had to get on with their own lives and help Lucy get on with hers. J.R. was who he was, but he was also one of them, and nobody could prove he'd done anything wrong.

Pam took Bobby's hand and squeezed it tightly. She knew that with Gary and Valene out of the way, J.R. would be coming after her before too long. Could she save her marriage? She knew how much Bobby loved her, but she didn't underestimate J.R.'s ability to sow havoc and destruction. She had seen first-hand how devious and destructive he could be. It was going to be a rough row to hoe.

Lucy ran outside into the fresh air, gulping and

gasping it into her lungs. Her whole body felt burned, as if it were on fire with the awful knowledge she had been given. She hated her parents at that moment even more than she hated J.R. How could they have abandoned her like that? And what would she do now?

Off in the distance she saw Ray Krebbs riding the range in his jeep. She waved him to pull over. Good old Ray Krebbs, the only person at Southfork who had never done her wrong, who had always been her friend. At least there was someone she could talk to.

He pulled over to pick her up, and they rode off. After she had poured out her heart to him, he stared into the distance for a long time. "Lucy," he said, "I only met your parents for a little while, but I have to tell you—I don't believe it. No matter what J.R. says. I just don't believe they'd haul off and leave you like that if they didn't have to. My advice to you is to hang loose and wait. I'll bet you that after a while, they'll get word to you. Believe me, the truth about all this is gonna come out someday. Truth always comes out, no matter how much dirt and lies you cover it over with. You're gonna be all right, kid. I just know it."

She hugged him as hard as she could. Her only friend in the whole wide world. Maybe he was right. He *had* to be right. He just had to.

The sun was about to set, and now it sent its rays through the clouds in a glorious sunburst. Lucy saw it, and to her it felt like a sign from heaven—a sign that things were, indeed, going to be all right. Yes, they surely were...

SOAPS & SERIALS™—a new genre of paperback books

THE YOUNG AND THE RESTLESS
DAYS OF OUR LIVES
GUIDING LIGHT
ANOTHER WORLD
AS THE WORLD TURNS
DALLAS™
KNOTS LANDING™
CAPITOL™

Every month—a *new* book in *each* series—in your local supermarket or bookstore or in the book section of drug stores, department stores and convenience stores. Ask for ***SOAPS & SERIALS***™ wherever paperback books are sold. If your local stores don't yet have ***SOAPS & SERIALS***™, let us know.

For back issues of books in any of our series, write to: